A MOTHER'S PLEA

A CHANCY ROSMAN WESTERN ADVENTURE
BOOK 3

Russell J. Atwater

Contents

Chapter 1
An Unlikely Hero

Finally, Betsy Slayton thought. She'd always imagined herself growing up and having a large family, and nothing in her determined spirit had changed. But after dinner, baths, and bedtime stories for her two younger siblings, she realized she wouldn't mind putting off children just a few years longer.

Billy, two, and Paul, four, were a delight around the house, and she spent no small part of her day chasing after the two rambunctious boys. Her mother said that, since Betsy was still only seventeen (*for one more month,* she smiled to herself), she had more energy and could keep up with "the rascals," as her stepfather, Chancy Rosman, liked to call the boys.

Chancy and her mother, Teresa, had been married for well-nigh five years at this point. Betsy had always enjoyed having the man as a boarder back when he'd first shown up, even if he seemed to ignore the lessons in proper grammar she tried to give him.

It seemed like ages ago now, but every time she heard him say "ain't," she knew she'd met a person with an even more stubborn nature than she herself had. Her mother always joked that she didn't know what to do with the pair of them, but all three would—*five, she corrected herself*—wouldn't know what to do without one another.

Chancy had been trouble from the moment he showed up, according to her mother. But Betsy knew what she really meant was that she cared for the man almost immediately. And he did nothing to allay those worries for the first year or two.

First a bounty hunter, then a sheriff. It had taken a long time for Teresa to convince the man to hang up his guns and embrace a slower pace of life.

Funny, Betsy thought. All the times they'd been hoping Chancy would put his guns away and now, tonight of all nights, it was all she could think about. It wasn't the first time they had left her at home with the boys, not by a long shot.

But something about this particular night, when her mother and Chancy had walked out to the barn, she'd had to stifle a request for them to come back, to not leave her alone.

The neediness was off-putting to her. She was independent, and there wasn't exactly anything she could put her finger on that made her feel so jittery. But something was off. *Probably just a storm rolling in*, she'd told herself.

But there were the riders. And out where they lived, that usually meant someone on the way to visit. These men, though, assuming it even was the same men over the last few days, had seemed to wander past, as if getting the lay of the land.

Even that was pointless, though. Chancy had been a rancher in the past, Teresa had reasoned. There was no sense in not settling down with her and Betsy and taking up the job again. And take it up, he had. Most of what she could see in any direction was, or soon would be, their land.

"And then I won't have to worry about you getting shot at all the time," her mother had said.

"Oh, don't worry." Chancy had grinned. "There's plenty of cattle rustlers in Nebraska."

Her mother had swatted at him, as she was prone to do, and the two had laughed, knowing full well that, while Chancy stood for what was just and right, he also had become a family man, whether he liked to admit the existence of a soft spot in himself or not.

And maybe that's exactly what it was. Betsy had noticed a handful of unfamiliar faces in town the last time she'd been down to the Nicholses' store. But that couldn't be it either. People passed through every day. It was part of the life and a big part of the town's economy.

So why had these three stuck out to her? It wasn't anything she could put her finger on, but her gut. It had had plenty to say. And in particular, it said, "Stay away! These guys are bad news."

Betsy looked out the front windows, thoughts of nameless bandits racing around her head like the swift animals of the outlaws. But what could they want with them, really? Unless, of course…

She thought back to Chancy's last case. A man had come seemingly from nowhere, looking to avenge a death. Was it so unlikely there was more than one family with an ax to grind regarding the bounty hunter?

She scanned the horizon and, just to ease her mind, double-checked the locks on the doors. If anyone wanted anything from them, it wouldn't be in the house.

Besides, she said to herself, the whole idea was silly. When someone came to the house, riding a horse to froth especially, it was because they needed help.

Chancy may have retired, but that didn't keep the people from looking to him when they weren't sure what to do. And she certainly didn't want to be standing in the way of helping someone in town in their moment of need, even if all she could do was direct them to where Chancy was.

Pushing the thoughts aside, she flounced into a chair in the living room. Not so very long ago, this would've been a boarding room, but it turned out Chancy had a real knack for ranching. That, along with hefty savings from past bounties he'd been lugging around in one of his trunks, had allowed the Slaytons to take down the "Rooms to Let" sign once and for all.

At first, Betsy thought it would be strange. She'd grown up with the constant influx of visitors, some just overnighters passing through, others looking to give life in Elkhorn a go.

A few were still about. In fact, their closest neighbors, Mr. Saunders and his son, Fred, had been the very first two to stay in the house, though Betsy and Fred both had been much too young to remember it.

The story her mother liked to tell was that Betsy and Fred, only two and three at the time, had taken an immediate liking to one another, and that was why Mr. Saunders claimed he had to stay.

"Looks like I'm not gonna be able to pull my boy away from that girl of yours," he'd supposedly said. "Guess we better look for something permanent."

Mr. Saunders had lost his wife during Fred's childbirth, and Betsy's father had passed before she was old enough to remember him. For a time, she'd thought her mother and Mr. Saunders would wed themselves, giving her a best friend and a brother all at once, but Mr. Saunders had found himself a wife in Jacqueline Smith, a local seamstress, and Fred had run with the rest of the boys. It didn't preclude visits fairly regularly, as Teresa and lately Chancy had both liked to point out.

But... Betsy sighed to herself. There would be plenty of time for men and children in her future. For now, it was, as always, books that held her greatest interest.

And now that the rascals were asleep, or at least were for a few minutes, she finally had a moment's peace to give to her reading. Most nights would've found her poring over schoolbooks. She was well beyond what the local schoolmarm offered as far as instruction was concerned, but the woman was a godsend with getting books through the mail and had quite the respectable library in her own home.

Betsy had spent plenty of long, cozy afternoons working through texts, sometimes she and Miss Buckley both scratching their heads over a particularly confusing portion.

Tonight, though, tonight was simply reading for the sheer joy of it. Through a bookseller acquaintance of Miss Buckley, they'd finally been able to get a copy of *The Strange Case of Dr. Jekyll and Mr. Hyde* by Robert Louis Stevenson. It had only been out a few months, but had already been causing quite a stir.

Teresa wasn't against fiction by any means, and Betsy herself had read a handful of the author's other books (though truth be told, she had mostly filed them away as books the boys might like later on). Still, there was something downright spooky about it. Maybe it wasn't the best book to read while her parents were off having a dinner and cards evening across town, but she just couldn't resist.

She turned the wick up on the oil lamp, knowing she'd more than once lost herself in a book and read till the sun went down, squinting at the pages until someone had come in and brought her back to reality. Tonight, there would be no distractions. She opened the volume, placing her cloth bookmark on the end table beside her, and dived in.

Before she could even finish the first paragraph, though, something caught her attention.

Horses.

More than one horse, her ear told her. And moving quickly. She'd been around enough animals in her seventeen years to read the sounds as easy as looking out the window. Plus, where the house sat, few visitors came out unannounced, especially not in such a hurry.

She slipped the marker back between the pages and moved to the front window.

Sure enough, three horses were leaving a dust cloud as they raced down the dirt track toward the ranch. It wasn't unheard of, she supposed. Despite Chancy having turned the sheriff's office over to Jack Wallace before marrying her mother, the occasional case still came his way.

"Purely on a consultation type way," he'd always told them both.

And he'd kept his word. For the most part.

This didn't seem like a typical visit, though. More like an emergency, judging by the pace. She went over to the door and stepped out on the front porch, hoping to save the men time by telling them where to find her stepfather before going through the unnecessary pleasantries.

Besides, the last thing she needed was Billy and Paul to wake up.

She walked out a bit onto the front path, raising her arm to the riders, though they made no effort to slow until they were practically on top of her.

The wind carried their dusty wake right on their heels, blowing around her as the horses skittered to a halt.

She coughed, waving the air away from her face. "Judging by the rush, you boys don't wanna linger here too long," she said.

The horses danced around her, skittish, forming a little circle with her at the center. "We're lookin' for Rosman," one of the young men said from her side.

Betsy looked over at him. He wasn't quite a young man, she supposed, though not exactly grown-up yet either. Somewhere in the middle ground. Twenty-five? Thirty? They all looked similar, all around the same age, and it didn't take her long to peg them as brothers. "He headed in to town with Mother," she said. "That's what I was coming to tell you before you dusted me out." She coughed into her sleeve.

"What're you tellin' us for?" a second one said. "He leave a message?"

"No," Betsy said, already exasperated. She intended to just pass on the information and head back inside. Now she was going to need to dust off her dress *and* check on the rascals before getting back to her book. "But I assumed the way you came tearing up the road, you were in trouble. He's at the Wallaces' tonight. You can find him there."

"Jack Wallace is the sheriff," one of the young men said to the others. "We don't need to be ridin' up in there."

"Why not?" Betsy said, annoyed to be wasting time but also feeling the first bit of unease.

"Well, now what?" one of them said, ignoring Betsy completely. "You said we'd have this taken care of tonight." Betsy looked back and forth between the two she could see, now terribly aware of the fact that the third was directly behind her.

The man on her left grinned. "I got an idea."

Betsy felt her stomach sink. She could try to run, but where? And what good would it do? She knew where the guns were in the house, and Chancy had given her more lessons than even she thought necessary on how to use them. But how to get to the house? No amount of learning would make her run faster than a horse, let alone three of them.

"He may actually be back shortly," she said, hearing the quaver in her own voice. "They don't like to be out past sunset. And… and he's meeting with some other men, some of his old lawmen friends here tonight. Everyone should arrive shortly. I thought perhaps you were with them."

"Didja now?" the man on her right said. "That's funny. A second ago you seemed to act like he warn't gonna be back for a while now. You all by your lonesome here?"

Betsy looked around. She knew the lying was pointless, but she had no other option. "No, of course not. You think he'd be inconsiderate enough to leave me alone? He always has one of his deputies stay when they go to town. He's out in the barn right now, actually. I can get him for you."

For the shortest moment, the gambit seemed to work. Then she felt the man behind her bring his horse up close. The animal's breath was at her ear, and she could feel the heat from its body on her back.

"I think we got all we need here," he said, obviously leaning in the saddle to speak quietly, close to her.

She told herself she wouldn't cry, wouldn't scream other than to get attention. But she also knew, out on the edge of town like they were, even screaming might not do much good.

"You sure?" the man on her left said.

"I ain't leaving empty-handed." She felt his grip on her arm like iron. "Besides, we deserve a little fun."

With that, he jerked her up onto the horse, the saddle horn digging painfully into her ribs. Before she could fight him, he'd pinned her arms behind her back, yanking a rope around her wrists and cinched the knot down tight.

"I'd tell ya not to make a fuss," he said, laughing as he pulled her body up farther onto the horse, bending her in half across the animal's back, "but it ain't gonna make any difference no which way."

The horse's spine pushed into her stomach, making it hard to breathe. She didn't even want to imagine what a ride, much less a gallop, would do to her insides. *But,* she thought coldly, *he was right.* A fuss wouldn't help at all, unless she wanted to fall under the running hooves of the horse.

Then again, maybe that would be better than what these three had planned.

"C'mon, boy!" the rider yelled over her. "Let's go have us a party!"

He spurred the animal heartlessly. Its whinny of pain was loud in her ears, and the animal took off at a run. Her intuition left her, and her fear was blotted out as the pain of the ride pounded into her.

***

Fred Saunders was tired. It had been a full day on the farm. Most of the planting had long been done, but every farm boy knew that was only one of a thousand tasks waiting every morning when the sun came up. Plant, weed, water, tend.

"Tend" was the worst, an all-encompassing term that meant many things, none of which were usually particularly enjoyable. But a man's gotta eat, as he'd heard so many times from his father.

Life on the Saunders farm wasn't bad. Or at least not any worse than anywhere else, he figured. They had a respectable spread, could sell off crops and put some money away, even hire a hand or two to help when things got *really* busy around harvest time. But that didn't make the warm days any shorter.

And it's only May, he thought. The winter had been mild, a blessing at the time, but as his pop and Ben Franklin's almanac warned, mild winters had a way of flying the flag for a long, hot, dusty summer.

The winds had already given his cheeks a burn that matched anything the sun had done in the past. The gritty air was like sand, and constantly wiping sweat away had given him raw patches across his forehead and under his eyes.

In all reality, he probably looked a right mess. But it wasn't as if Betsy hadn't seen him that way before. Still, over the last year or so, he'd cared a lot more about what the blond girl up the road thought about his appearance.

He'd known Betsy for so long, he'd almost never thought of her as a girl. She was just always there, like a sister, he supposed. He'd gone to her for help with schooling, had their handful of adventures when they were younger, but something had changed over the last twelve months, and he didn't know what to think of it.

Not that she'd grown up. He'd seen her grow up the same as he had been doing. But it was like he was *noticing* it for the first time. She wasn't just the gangly firecracker he would pal around with anymore.

She had the curves of a young woman. And the beautiful long hair. She wore it up mostly, said she didn't want to look like a tart. But he'd seen her around the ranch often enough, big curls falling around her shoulders, and, well, it did something to him.

He adjusted his hat on his head, wincing as the brim brushed along the raw skin on his forehead. He probably looked like he'd been dragged behind the horse instead of riding it over. But he wanted to see her, and his work was done for the day, so there wasn't any gosh darn reason he couldn't just go say hello. He'd done it a thousand times before. Ten thousand, probably.

Up ahead, just past the crossroads where he needed to take a left, a cloud of dust curled up in the air. Riders heading out to the Rosman place, by the look of it. For its locale, they got more visitors than one might expect, but ever since Chancy had up and married Teresa, that wasn't entirely out of the ordinary. He was a big man in town. Even Fred remembered when Harman Swally had gone down, and before that, the McFarland fella.

To be honest, if he hadn't known Chancy for so long, he'd be near intimidated before heading over to see Betsy. A small part of him still was.

He tried to shake the feeling. If Chancy was busy, then he could still see Betsy and maybe be a little more relaxed about it.

Then again, if Chancy headed into town—even worse, if Chancy *and* Teresa headed into town—it wouldn't be right for him to be hanging around with Betsy, just the two of them. Sure, the boys would be there, but—he glanced at the sky—they were probably bedding down for the night, if they hadn't already. And despite what he knew to the contrary, no one seemed to believe a four-year-old made a good chaperone.

He nudged the horse into a trot, keeping an eye over toward the ranch. The riders had stopped and seemed to mill about in front of the house. The boys must've been in bed, he thought. Chancy'd gone out to meet the men before they could wake the children and likely earn him a good tongue-lashing from Teresa.

He couldn't see precisely what was going on, some kind of chitchat, though something in his gut told him it didn't look quite right. The horses seemed jittery, even at this distance. The animals moved back and forth, never seeming to stand still.

He'd seen it before in the past. Usually, it was the sign of an unsure rider, the horse feeling the nervousness of the man on its bad. It also happened when a skittish animal got startled, or was kept that way. The manner in which they moved was almost like something was between them all.

Fred had assumed it was Chancy, but that man had a way of making everybody

feel comfortable, man or beast, right until he decided not to.

As Fred watched, one man, the one closest to the house, pulled something up onto his saddle, made a few quick motions, and the three animals turned to leave in a clatter of hooves.

He nudged his own horse up to a canter. Something wasn't right, but he didn't want to overreact. He leaned forward in the saddle, straining his eyes in the dying light.

That was when he saw it.

A flash of gold.

Fred kicked the horse into a gallop, muttering an apology to the already tired animal, but that color could only be one thing. If he was wrong, well, he'd make a fool of himself and deal with it later. But his heart felt cold, and he focused his brain on only one thing: getting to Betsy.

Fred raced along the hundred yards between him and the crossroads, knowing he'd have a better chance of keeping the situation detained if the three other avenues of escape weren't easy to get to. How he was going to fight off three men never crossed his mind.

Instead, he merely registered the feel of his six-shooter in his hand. His father had given it to him two years ago, a birthday present. He had thought little of it. There was little action in the bean-field each day, but he'd liked the feel and taken to wearing it every day. Now, he couldn't be more grateful for the gift.

Fred hit the crossroads first, reining in the horse only enough to make a sliding, slipping turn onto the path that led to the Rosman ranch, toward Betsy.

Ahead of him, the riders seemed to notice his presence for the first time. There was a minimal effort at spreading out, but the narrow road made it difficult. Chancy had run wire fencing all along his property over the years. Somewhere in the back of his mind, Fred remembered helping do that. Initially, it was to keep livestock *in* the fields. Now, he was grimly happy to see, it also kept critters *out.*

Fred held his gun up and fired once into the air, reining in his horse and turning sideways in the road. It was foolish. Three against one. They may as well just ride him down as anything, but he had no other options.

He could now see the bundle on the rear horse. It was Betsy, kicking her legs, being bounced around like a drop of water on a hot skillet.

Fred lowered his gun, aiming deliberately. For a second, he wondered if he should order them to stop, tell them he would shoot. But the gesture was apparently clear enough. A shot cracked out from the trio, harmlessly kicking up dirt down the road behind him, but it was enough to get Fred moving.

Sitting motionless on the road had been as foolish as they come, he realized. Why give them a stationary target when he had three moving ones to deal with?

He jerked at the reins, the animal beneath him seeming more than ready to move, flee if possible. He'd never tested her in a situation like this, but it was clearly going to be a trial by fire.

He raced down the road a few paces, trying to increase the space as best he could, perhaps give his pursuers the false hope that he was fleeing. Then, abruptly, he jerked the reins, pulling the animal around and charging straight back toward the gang.

The surprise worked only for a moment, but it was enough for him to squeeze off one good shot. The man on the left flipped back out of his saddle, the yelp of pain audible even over the cacophony of trampling hooves and gunfire. His two companions seemed to hesitate for a moment, almost as if they weren't sure whether or not to leave him.

Good, Fred thought. *If they won't look out for each other, I may just have a chance.*

The other two yelled at one another for a second, arguing about something. Before, just as he hoped, the man on the right spurred his horse and cut out toward the fields. It was the one thing Fred was hoping they wouldn't try. Visually, the fence was a deterrent, but only to the animals who weren't wise enough to realize they could easily break through. On a galloping horse, it was only a nuisance to spring over. Which was just what the fleeing man did, cutting out through the prairie toward escape.

Good riddance, Fred thought. *That's two down.*

Up ahead, he saw what he hadn't had the courage to hope for. The man on the horse carrying Betsy jumped out of the saddle and raced over to his fallen companion. Fred slowed his own animal, not wanting to race into any kind of shoot-out while Betsy was in the middle of it all.

The two men struggled to rise. *Damn, must've only winged him.* The pair stumbled over toward the remaining horse, one helping the other up onto the saddle and them climbing on behind him, leaving Betsy to lie where she was.

It was good, very good. But not great. That left only one exit, as there was no way any horse was going to jump a fence with two grown men on its back.

Fred brought his animal to a standstill, knowing this was going to be the moment he lived or died. His mind flashed back to pictures of knights he'd seen as a boy. Two men racing at one another with nowhere to go but forward.

Now, instead of one chance with a lance, though, they had however many shots could be fired in the fleeting seconds.

With no time to reload, Fred hoped the advantage of a larger target would come to his aid. The horse ahead of him reared slightly, appearing more inclined to throw both the men than race off with them. But they held firm and within seconds were barreling down on him.

Fred tried to remember what he'd learned. Lead the target. Squeeze the trigger, don't pull. He aimed just ahead of the men, hoping he didn't plug the horse by mistake, but knowing whatever brought them down would have to work. A shot came back at him, his focus so intense he barely noticed as the slug ripped through his shirt sleeve, just grazing the skin beneath.

He timed the animal's movement, counting on the rhythmic gallop to make his shot work for him. He breathed out slowly, squeezed the trigger.

The crack of the gun was loud, and he was sure his shot was true.

But there was no kick in his hand, no buck of the revolver as the gunpowder let loose. Instead, almost as if time had slowed, he felt a punch in his chest, a searing pain. Something shattered. The bullet tore out his back. Its impact knocked him backward out of the saddle.

He felt the animal's rump on his back, the way the horse twisted, leaping out from under him. He twisted as he fell, landing face first in the dirt. He heard, almost far off, shots, hooves galloping. Dirt kicked up. From bullets or horseshoes, he couldn't tell which, but he felt the animal race by more than anything, the ground seeming to jar his body, set fire to his wounds. Things grew dim, the world spinning, getting hazy, dark.

Fred could see the horse with its two riders disappearing in a cloud of dust, making the way to the crossroads, turning, getting smaller, smaller.

He fought against it. *Betsy!* He had to get to Betsy. She was close, maybe hurt.

He tried to push up off the ground, crying out as he put weight on his left arm and crumpling back into the dirt. His chest heaved, but even that movement brought so much pain, he felt himself growing lightheaded again.

No, he thought. *No, not now.*

He had to find Betsy first. Then if he passed out, if he died, so be it. But not until he knew she was safe.

Gritting his teeth, favoring his right arm, he struggled up to a kneeling position. His horse, despite the scare, hadn't run far. The animal sauntered back, almost sensing his need for her.

She was a splendid animal, he thought. He should tell her that...

He shook his head, trying to keep his thoughts clear. In front of him dangled a stirrup. He reached out, grasping the iron rod that had supported his boot so often, and yanked, pulling himself up to one foot, both feet, and slowly, excruciatingly slowly, worked his way to a standing position.

The sweat on his forehead was cold, running in rivulets from his brow, down his cheeks into his eyes, burning in the raw places of his skin.

He took a deep breath, trying to ignore the heat that brought to his shoulder and chest. "Betsy!"

It hurt, badly. He felt like he could taste blood, but in the dust and pain, he could hardly trust his senses. Instead, he needed to act.

He took a few steps forward, the animal almost seeming to understand and moving with him, giving him something to lean against as they covered the twenty yards. All that had stood between him and the girl all along.

It seemed so much farther, he thought. Then again, twenty yards with a six-shooter wasn't exactly a guarantee by any means, given his marksmanship. The first shot must've been a fluke, giving him false confidence.

"May as well have shot 'em all in the air," he gasped to the horse, trying to keep talking and stay conscious.

Ahead, he could hear Betsy calling his name. She sounded scared, but not afraid. She couldn't be. He had chased the men away.

Maybe they were coming back. He turned slightly, trying to glance over his shoulder but losing his balance and stumbling against the horse. It whinnied at him, but stayed by his side.

He heard the whoosh of fabric and a bump as Betsy must have rolled herself out of the saddle.

Not a very safe move. She could hurt herself. Break an arm even. He chuckled a little to himself. Wouldn't they be a pair? Both with broken arms. Because surely that was all this could be, right? Just a broken arm. It happened to folks all the time. Doc would fix him up.

The horse stopped moving beside him, though his own feet didn't react quickly enough, and he stumbled forward, attempting to catch himself but immediately letting out a cry of pain and falling down in the dust again as his injured arm had ever so briefly attempted to support his weight.

"Fred!"

He could hear her voice before he could see her, hear her struggling to stand then hurrying to him.

"Fred I need your help," she said, leaning close. "We're going to be okay, but my hands are tied. I need you to help me. Can you do that?"

He started to reply, but the words felt stuck in his throat. He shook his head, focusing on the pain, forcing himself to come back to reality. Betsy needed him. He had to be there for her. He took a deep breath, wincing but almost savoring the pain. "Are you," he coughed, "are you okay?"

"I'm fine, Fred." She sounded calm, but he could hear something else in her voice. He knew her too well for her to hide things from him.

"Is it pretty bad?" he said.

"It's not your best look, Fred." She tried to laugh. "But it'll be okay. I need your help first, though. I need you to help me with these knots."

He reached out with his right hand, fumbled once, and knew it was hopeless for him to attempt any kind of simple motion like that.

"You can do it, Fred, I know you can. Just help me a little. We can do it together."

"No." He pulled his hand back, fighting to shove it in the pocket of his trousers. His fingers were slick. So much blood. They found what he wanted, slipped again.

He took a painful breath, trying to calm himself, and slowly pulled a small pocketknife from his pants. He held it up to his mouth with his good hand, using his teeth to pry open the blade. "Careful," he said, placing the knife in her hand so the blade faced the ropes and the handle was within her firm grasp.

"Oh, Fred." He could hear the joy in her voice. Real joy. Because of him. "You're amazing, just amazing. You keep talking to me, okay? As soon as I get these ropes cut, we're gonna have to get you up to the house. Now, don't you go scaring the boys either. They're trying to sleep. Are you hearing me, Fred? This is a right mess, but it would've been so much worse without you. You really are a hero…"

He heard a gasp of happiness as she, he assumed, cut through the ropes. That was good. He could rest now. Betsy was safe. He could rest now and things would be okay…

Chapter 2
Family

Chancy Rosman had hung up his guns years before. It seemed like a lifetime ago, but some habits had gotten into his bones. The alertness and keen eye he'd developed over the years had made him successful as both a bounty hunter and a sheriff.

They were the things that had kept him alive on several occasions. Sometimes he wondered what it would be like to go through a day without being aware of every sound on the wind, the play of shadows, the lilts and timbre of voices overwhelming him with information. Most times, after this long, he could filter out the usual and let normal parts of the day slip by.

As he and Teresa rode slowly back up the dirt road toward their home, something tickled at the back of his mind. The sun had long since set, but some low layer of his mind must have noticed the play of dark shadows in the dirt, the scuffle of hoofprints at the crossroads. Before Teresa seemed aware anything could be amiss, he noticed the smell of sweat in the air. Sweat and blood.

Up ahead, if he strained, he could make out a dark form on the road and, without a moment's hesitation, spurred his horse to a gallop, bolting away from Teresa mid-sentence.

He heard her call his name behind him, but his calculating mind also knew there was no trouble at the rear of them. He'd paid attention on the ride back, as always. Whatever was happening was just ahead. And Teresa wasn't the type to hang back and wonder, either. He could hear her horse whinny and take up the chase seconds later.

The glow of the moon played on the bodies ahead of him, though he could already distinguish the larger forms. A horse off to one side. A person, no two people, on the road. One lying flat, one kneeling above.

The wind blew from behind him, preventing the usual carrying of voices, but the starlight shined bright enough in the open expanse to show the glint of blond hair in the night.

"Betsy!" he called out, more to let the girl know who was coming than to assess her situation. Whatever was going on, she was in better shape than the body before her. She was at least moving.

He saw her look up and wave her arms, heard a cry from Teresa behind him as she recognized the subtle, unique movements only mothers seem to pick up on. The little nuances that made Betsy her child.

Chancy pulled back hard on the reins, the horse already sensing the stop and bracing its hooves as it skid in the dirt. Before the animal had stopped moving, Chancy was out of the saddle, down on a knee beside the girl.

"It's Fred!" she cried.

There was blood on her hands, smeared across her forehead from where she'd wiped sweat away. Tears ran down her cheek, leaving little trails in the dust on her cheeks.

All of this in a quick glance, and Chancy knew, at least physically, Betsy was okay. She was moving naturally, if erratically. She was clear-headed. Traumatized later maybe, but then again, not everyone was as used to the dead and dying as a bounty hunter.

And it was the Saunders boy, not just somebody. The young man had been around ever since Chancy could remember.

Gently yet firmly, Chancy folded Betsy's hands and put them in her lap. Teresa rode up moments later, and Chancy knew she would tend to the girl.

He looked down at Fred. A gunshot wound.

No. Two.

The one didn't look so bad. A graze. Maybe needed some stitching up if the doc went that route, though the local fella didn't seem so crazy about the procedure as some Chancy had met.

It was the bullet hole in his chest that had Chancy concerned. More than concerned, really. Losing all hope felt more accurate.

Blood pumped out freely now that Betsy's hands weren't holding it in, and Chancy jerked off his light evening jacket, balling it up and shoving it under the boy's back. If the entry wound looked like this, it didn't bode well for the other side. Time was ticking, and feeling the tacky dirt as he rolled the boy over, he was afraid too much may have already gone by.

"Teresa!"

He didn't shout, not exactly. But it was a voice of authority. The mother and daughter were rightly scared for one another, but he couldn't allow them to get caught up in their emotions just yet. Right now, he needed action.

"I need Betsy with me. She'll be safe. You get on that horse and get the doc. Now!"

He could see the moment's hesitation flit across the woman's face. Chancy could easily guess her thoughts. Whatever had happened to her daughter happened while she was gone, while no one was there to protect her. No matter how old Betsy got, she was still her mother's child. But he could also easily guess what would happen to Fred if people didn't get moving.

"I need Betsy here," he said in a softer, though still firm, tone. "Go. Now!"

Teresa nodded, kissed the girl on the forehead and looked her in the eyes. "I'll be right back. You're safe. Just stay with Chancy. You're safe."

The girl, showing a grit Chancy couldn't help but admire, tilted her head quickly and almost shooed her mother away.

As Teresa rode for help, Chancy did the best he could to coax Betsy through what happened. It seemed obvious to him from the start that the boys were okay. Even Teresa appeared to know on some level that, were anything amiss, Betsy would've been at the house or at the very least immediately mentioned the rascals.

Chancy looked at the girl. Her hands were shaking, and she was pale, even in the night's dim light, but she was fighting to stay with him. She'd never been one to shy away from a problem. He'd seen that in her more than once, but this was more than a problem. Sure, people died out their way, but it wasn't usually your friend. And if Chancy guessed correctly, they rarely died protecting you.

"I want you to do two things for me," he said, fixing his gaze directly on the girl's eyes, keeping her attention focused on him. "Pay attention."

She nodded her head up and down once, quickly.

"Go into the house and check on the boys. They may be awake and wondering where everybody is. If they are, just tell them we're back and everything is okay. Don't spook 'em, okay? Just say, 'Mom and Chancy are back and everything's okay.'"

She nodded again.

"Then get the blanket off the couch and a pitcher of water and come straight back."

She nodded a third time, though he could see her gaze slipping back toward Fred's body.

"Betsy. Say it back to me."

"Mom and Chancy are back and everything's okay," she said mechanically.

"And?" She looked at him.

"C'mon, Betsy. Fred needs you."

The name appeared to bring her back to her senses. Her eyes cleared, and she jumped to her feet. "Everything's okay, and you need blankets and water."

"Good girl," he said.

As Betsy raced off toward the house, Chancy began talking to the boy, keeping pressure on the bullet hole and praying the two women would return with help soon.

***

The following morning, Chancy was still awake, standing out on the porch and looking out into the distance. A cup of coffee steamed on the porch rail by his hand.

After Teresa had gotten back, Chancy had helped load Fred into a wagon and rode back to the doctor's office with the man, spending the better part of four hours there. He knew it was of little help, but he also knew his wife and daughter needed time together before he came back.

Shoot, he knew he needed time away before he tried to speak with them.

He'd changed over the years, settled down, some might say. But this was his family. His home. At the moment he'd realized Betsy was the one kneeling in the road, all of his old anger for justice and vengeance came pouring back. Being around the women would only intensify it, and that wasn't what they needed. Not at that moment.

About half an hour before sunup, the doctor had walked out of his back room, wiping blood off his hands on a handkerchief. Chancy had been around enough gunfights to know Fred's odds weren't good to begin with.

The bullet had only missed his heart by pure luck. But a shot like that, especially lying in the road and waiting for help like he'd had to do… When the doctor shook his head, there wasn't the least bit of surprise.

"Thanks, Doc," Chancy said.

"He'd just lost too much blood already," the doctor said. "There was nothing I could do."

Chancy nodded and turned toward the door, preparing himself for the next task on his list. The Saunders' were a reliable couple, the type folks said you could set your watch by. What that meant now was they were probably unaware anything amiss had even occurred. They went to bed early. Fred had mentioned more than once on his evening visits that they hit the hay as soon as the sun went down.

Now, not only did they likely not even know their son wasn't at home, Chancy had the job to tell them he'd never be coming back.

It had gone about like he'd expected.

He heard the door open and close behind him and felt Teresa's arms at his waist, her head leaning against his back.

"How is she?" he said.

He felt her sigh into him. "Okay," she said. "Like you might expect. I don't know, Chancy. She's safe. She's not hurt, at least, not in the ways I'm sure they intended. I just don't know why it would happen to her. Of all people."

"It's dangerous out here, Rees. I think we forget that sometimes."

"No." She turned him around to face her. "I don't know 'why her' like some kind of philosophy question. I mean, why *her?* She's your daughter, for goodness' sake. Everyone knows that. What kind of fool would come after Chancy Rosman's family?"

He wanted to feel proud of the statement. And there was a small part of him that felt confident she trusted him to such a high extent. But the thing was… what made her feel safe was often what put her and the kids in danger. It was one reason he'd stayed on his own for so long. When a man has nothing to lose, he's practically invincible. Now he had four things that could be taken from him.

He put his hands on her shoulders and looked her in the eye. "I understand what you're saying. But the fact is, the list of people who would come after you all is probably a lot longer than either of us cares to think about. I've spurned a lotta people in my time. What you've seen over the years barely scratches the surface."

"But you're not the sheriff anymore. You're not a bounty hunter. It's been years since you've ridden out like you used to. Surely if something were going to happen, it would've happened before now. Don't you think? It's been so long." Her eyes pleaded with him to agree, even though he felt like she knew as well as he did that time never really healed all wounds. Especially when vengeance was involved.

"You might be right," he conceded. "It could be random. Despite what you like to believe, the name Chancy Rosman really ain't so well known as folks here seem to say. And we get plenty of folks passing through onto other parts. This house sitting out like it does. Well, maybe we just looked like an easy target. What all did she tell you?"

"Just that the boys were in bed and some riders came up. She figured they were looking for you, so she went out to send 'em on before she woke the young ones."

"Then they sprung."

"Then they sprung." There was a hitch in her voice at the last word. He could see she was trying her best to stay strong, but there was a mix of emotions in her that made keeping any of them in check a hard task. Wrangling all of them at once was beyond anyone's ability. "They tried to *take* her, Chancy! Like they were stealing chickens!"

"I know." He pulled her in, wanting to comfort her with the feeling of safety another body could provide, but she pushed him back.

"No," she said, her hands on his chest. "I don't want to feel okay now. I don't want to be happy she's here. Lord knows I am. But the Lord also knows what I really feel is mad. I'm angry, Chancy. This is your home, too, you know. How can you stand there so calm? Like… like it's just another horse that threw a shoe or a broken plowshare? This is your *family* they tried to take. Your *daughter*."

Chancy clenched his teeth. He couldn't argue with the woman. Didn't want to, even if he could. She was right. And truth be told, he was happy to see the rage boiling in her. It was the right reaction. There was a time for turning the other cheek. He'd heard that enough times to see the value in it.

But he also knew there were lines you don't cross. And this was miles over that line.

"I'll get to the bottom of it," he said finally. "This ain't just about us, after all."

"Oh, no." Teresa put her hands to her chest. "Oh my goodness. I didn't even think to ask. I'm horrible. Fred. How is he? Please tell me that poor boy is all right."

Chancy shook his head. "I just came back from their place."

The tears Teresa had been struggling to hold back for her own family found an escape when sympathy was involved. "He was only trying to help…" she whispered.

"He helped," Chancy said. "We owe that boy everything we got right now. He died a hero."

Teresa turned away. "But he still died! On our land. Protecting our family. He probably rode out thinking he might steal a few minutes with Betsy, and he ends up dead. Chancy, don't you see?"

"I see all right, Teresa. That's why, as soon as the sun comes up, I'm riding in to see Jack. He needs to know what's going on. I'd've headed over already, but I didn't want to leave you on your own." He paused. "And I'd like to talk to Betsy as well. When you think she's ready."

Teresa nodded, looking down at her hands. "She's resting now, though I don't know any time will be better than another for this. Perhaps it's best to just get it over with and help her move forward, rather than drag this out."

"Did she tell you anything?" he asked. "If she doesn't have much to say, I don't want to make things worse. I can just go see Jack now and let her rest."

"No," she said. "It's best we do this now, while it's fresh in her mind." The woman turned toward the door and then back to him. "Chancy, I know I told you that once you turned in the star we were done with that life. I know I begged you to do it. But I also know you keep those guns cleaned and oiled. Chancy – I'm pleading with you. I don't care what I said before. Strap those guns back on and end this now!"

Chancy looked at his wife. She'd never shied away from the violence his job entailed. She was aware of it from the first time he set foot in her boarding house so many years ago and had been dragged into it more than he'd ever imagined.

But once they'd wed, he'd done his best to leave all that behind him. It was something he had done for her, yes, but also something he had been prepared to do for a long time, he realized. It was as if there were two versions of him, and he'd grown to enjoy being the ranching man again. Sure, the pace of life was slower, but he also had a home for the first time in a long while. He had a family, people who cared about him for more than just his ability to track a man down.

"You're sure?" he said, knowing Teresa wouldn't have said anything if she hadn't been, but still wanting to give her one more chance.

"I've never been so sure, Chancy. Jack is a capable man. I know he and his deputies won't let us down. But this is beyond that. This is our family. It's our home. And it's us who need to send a clear message: don't come looking for trouble here, or you'll get it."

Chancy folded his arms, partly admiring the tenacity in the woman, partly letting the old coolness come back into his veins. Bounty hunting had been his life, but it wasn't a switch, something he could turn on and off.

"I do this, I'm all in. You know that, right? I don't know what will happen, but I know I won't stop till it's done. One way or the other."

Teresa looked up at him, her jaw set. "I'm good with that. That's what I'm counting on."

Chapter 3
The Carter Brothers

In the Shipyard's backroom, Ship Buchanon and a few of his closer clientele were whiling away the early morning, or for them, late night hours, around a small wooden table.

The man on his left was busy pressing the sharp end of a tack into playing cards, leaving a kind of bumped pattern that would allow any player with the right experience to read their backs as he dealt them out.

On his right, a fellow was filing down a lead fishing weight, gathering the shavings into a small pile, and carefully pouring them into a hole he'd just drilled into the "one" pip on a die.

Ship had never been foolish enough to control the gaming that happened in his saloon. It was going to happen whether or not he kept an eye on it, so he'd long treated it like any other aspect of the business. As long as it was making him money, he didn't look too much into it.

The crew in the backroom he mostly kept around out of habit. Most of them he'd known for well on twenty years, though Jasper, the fella weighting the dice, was actually the son of a man Ship used to ride with till that old coot caught a bullet in the back years ago. Seemed like the least he could do for Jasper was to help bring him up right.

Plus, he never liked to count out his money alone, and these were the few men he knew he could trust to have his back if someone decided count night would be a good time to make a move.

He put another stack of bills on his left, making a mark in his ledger. *It wasn't exactly honor among thieves*, he thought, *but it was close enough*. These boys were more averse to handouts and easy money, truth be told. Jasper himself had said it on several occasions.

"Anybody can shove a gun in your face, Ship. But then you avoid that feller, right? I figure you *lose* your money to me. Well, hell, I didn't do nothing but give you the chance to win mine. Them boys'll come back with their last penny and thank you for the opportunity. That's how you make money out here. Get 'em to give it to you, and they not only ain't mad, they're happy to give you more later on."

The kid had a point. The funny thing was, Ship thought, finding a straight game anywhere, but especially in this saloon, was about the hardest part of it. He knew there were plenty of places to sit down for faro in town. Shoot, he'd even seen some whist not too long ago, though the hoity-toity attitude was a little much for him.

It was something about the place, he'd finally decided. The risks might be higher, but then again, so were the payouts. "A gentleman's game" meant nothing here, and folks were prepared for that, or they wouldn't sit down at his tables.

He thought, moving another stack of bills to his left. It *was the drink that brought in the most. Well, the drink and the gals.* If Jasper wanted to keep running his crooked games, that was fine with Ship. As saloon owner, he was still pulling a ten percent cut either way.

The banging of the front door caused all three men to pause in their movements. It wasn't concern for the money, or being found out, but the sheer strangeness of anyone coming in at this unholy hour.

They said lawlessness never sleeps, but even Ship knew it sure seemed to get started later in the day. He shoved some cash bundles into a leather satchel at his feet and stood up, drawing his revolver and stepping toward the door.

There were sounds of scuffling, though not like a fight. Grunts, a knocked-over chair. Movement toward them. Jasper and his cohort stood and moved back from the table, giving themselves room for whatever was coming their way.

"Ship!" a voice called out.

"Oh, hell," the man said, shoving his gun back in his holster. "I shoulda knowed." He reached over and opened the door, gesturing for the other men to get settled again. This wasn't precisely what he'd expected, but he couldn't say the outcome overly surprised him.

"Back here," he called gruffly, holding the door open.

In the middle of the saloon stood the Carter brothers. Or at least two stood, supporting the third between them. They were filthy, dust-covered, and sweaty, but it did little to hide the blood pouring from the one in the middle.

"We need the doc," Matt said.

Ship sighed. "Bring him back here." He turned to the two men behind him. "Clear the table. One of you go up and see if the doc's awake."

Jasper gathered up his tools and slipped out while Marty shoved the deck in his pocket. "Man can't work in peace around here," Ship heard him mutter.

The three interlopers made their way across to the back room, bumping into a table on the way and knocking over two chairs. Ship hadn't seen them in years, at least not before earlier that day. They'd come in spitting fire and ready to raise hell.

He'd known better than to send them out to the Rosman place, but they were on a tirade about Bart. There used to be four Carter brothers. Bart, Matt, Ernie, and Evan. According to Matt, Rosman was the man who'd shot down Bart a few years back, and they were out for blood.

Ship didn't know if there was any truth to the story, but he attempted to ensure vendettas of that type weren't his concern at all. You get mixed up with folks like that. It becomes damn near impossible to run a half-respectable business.

The only reason the Shipyard had lasted like it had was that Ship's only alliance was to himself, and he made sure everybody who came through his doors knew that.

Not that he was heartless, in his own way. The old doc, at least that's what he'd been before the whiskey got the better of him, had slept on the bar many nights. Ship finally ended up letting the man use one of the spare rooms upstairs when he needed it.

Never hurt to have a doctor hEvan, after all. Especially when your closer acquaintances spent their time branding cards and loading dice. Seemed to increase the odds of gunplay, despite Jasper's positive theories.

Matt and Evan dragged Ernie back into the room, unceremoniously jerking his body up onto the table. His one arm hung uselessly at his side, blood dripping off his fingers and onto the floor. Given that he didn't cry out, gave more of a moan really, Ship wondered just how much blood the boy had lost on the way over. Rosman's place was on the other side of town, and given how far out and lonesome it sat, he was guessing the man was about bled dry. Even under the dust caked on his sweaty face, Ernie looked pale.

"Told you boys this'd happen," Ship said, leaning against the doorway.

"Warn't even him," Matt said, tossing his hat on the chair next to him. "Some young kid come up outta nowhere."

Ship glanced over at the stairs where Jasper was helping a bleary-looking doc down the steps. "Some kid, huh? Maybe you lucked out then."

Matt glared at him. "Rosman warn't even there. If he was, this'd all be over and done with by now."

Ship laughed. "I imagine that's truer'n you think."

It looked like the kid was about to say something again when Jasper and the doc elbowed by.

Ship glanced down at the doctor's shaking hands and looked over at Marty and jerked his head toward the bar. "Go grab a bottle of whiskey."

The card shark nodded and stepped out to the bar.

"Well…" the doctor said, clearing his throat and moving up to examine the wound. "Can't say it's the first time I've seen one of these." He almost tittered a bit, making Ship wonder if more whiskey was really the answer. *But*, he thought, *if the old coot was gonna be digging a bullet out of my shoulder, I'd prefer steady hands over a clear mind*. Lord knew Ship had seen the man do it blind drunk plenty of times.

"It ain't bad," Matt said to the old man. "Probably came out the other side, even."

The doctor looked up at him briefly, then began unbuttoning Ernie's shirt, spreading the material so he could see the pulsing, ragged hole. "Maybe it did, maybe it didn't." He jerked the material back over the shoulder and tilted the young man up on his side, trying to get a better view of the back.

Ship had never been squeamish about blood or death, but he had to admit, Ernie might be glad he was mostly unconscious for this part. The doc might have done this plenty of times, but with the experience came a gruffness of demeanor that looked more than a little painful. Then again, it might just be his annoyance at having been woken up for another "fool gunshot," as he had taken to calling them over the years.

"And it looks like maybe it didn't," the doc said, rolling the body farther and pressing his fingers around a discolored place on Ernie' back, just beside the shoulder blade. "But it's gonna have to here in a minute. Hey, boy." He looked at Jasper. "Run back up and grab my kit."

Jasper sighed and walked back toward the stairs.

"Thanks, boy." Ship grinned as the young man walked by. The doc could be Jasper's grandpa, he knew, but in this place, age became a lot more fluid. Sure, Jasper was young, younger than the Carters even, but to Ship, they were all kids.

Bart Carter had caught his bullet around thirty, Ship thought, putting these other fellows in their early twenties. Marty, well, Ship really didn't know how old the man was. He had one of those faces that defied guessing. Whatever the case, he'd always felt age was in how a man carried himself, and at this moment, the Carter brothers were acting like the youngest whippersnappers he'd seen in a while.

Matt blanched at the sight of the wound. Evan turned his head away.

"Look a lot different up close, don't they?" the doctor said, a little laugh slipping out again. "You boys never mind being the ones shooting, but you see what I have to do afterward? Feels like I've spent half my life digging bullets outta the likes of you."

"Just get it out," Matt said through gritted teeth.

Ship walked over and took Ernie by the arm, partly wanting to get the kid out of the room before he retched all over, partly wanting information more than he needed to see the surgery through. Ernie would either live or he wouldn't, and if he didn't, it's not like it would be the first body Ship had had in his saloon.

Looking more than a little relieved, Evan followed Ship out to the bar just as Jasper was coming back down the step with the leather doctor's kit. "No rest for the wicked, eh?"

Jasper tried to laugh as he passed the men and headed into the back room.

Ship deposited Evan on a barstool and walked around to pour a few beers. "So, what's the story here? Y'all didn't even see Rosman?"

The kid scratched at his armpit and adjusted the stool underneath him, trying to regain his composure. "Nah," he said. "Some biddy came out. Said he warn't there or some such rot. Matt got it in his head we'd just take the girl instead."

"Have a little fun with her, huh?"

"Naw, it warn't like that..." Evan trailed off.

He was the youngest of the group, or at least Ship was pretty sure that was the case. It was hard to keep track of who was running with who half the time. "You were just gonna hang onto her, huh?"

Evan shrugged. "I didn't have no intentions, if that's what you're implying." He paused for a moment before adding, "Can't say about the others."

Ship nodded. "Sounds about right. So," he set a mug of beer on the bar in front of the kid. "What happened then? You grabbed the girl, you said, but I don't see her nowheres."

"That's when this other feller came riding up," Evan said, holding onto the mug. "Don't know who he was or where in hell he came from. Just comes galloping up outta the dark, shot Ernie, caused holy hell with our plan. Matt dropped the gal to get Ernie, and we came here."

"And that's it, huh?"

"Far as what matters, I reckon it is."

Ship grinned. "You don't know the half of it, kid. If I'm guessing, you went after ole Betsy. She ain't Chancy's girl, not by blood, but she may as well be. Most likely it was the Saunders boy who run up on you. Those folks got a place out that way."

"He ain't a problem no more," Evan said. "Shot him clean outta the saddle."

This time Ship laughed. "Maybe *he* ain't a problem himself, but you boys just keep digging this hole deeper. I told you it was trouble to go after Rosman."

"It's one man," Evan said. "And he's *old.*"

Ship leaned on the bar, staring at the kid until he made eye contact. "Don't matter how old that man is," Ship said. "You ain't even seen him yet, and he's damn close to costing you two of your brothers. You think that's the type of fella who's gonna take lightly to you shooting up his neighbors and trying to ride off with his little girl?"

Evan shrugged. "Matt said it was three to one, no problem."

"Yeah, well, Matt ain't so tough as he'd like everybody to think, if you want my two cents."

The kid shrugged again. "Tough or not, it's gotta be done. It's about honor."

Ship laughed, tossing his head back and almost getting tears in his eyes. "Matt tell you that too? Say something about how you gotta do it for the family? Get vengeance for your brother? Well, listen, kid, there's something you need to hear right now and either make your peace with it or move along. There ain't no honor on this side of things. You leave that behind with your nappies. You wanna run with the big boys, you're gonna catch a bullet eventually. What do you think Rosman's gonna tell folks? He had it coming? You better be damn sure when he says it's about honor, folks'll believe it. Because for him, it is. You go after a man, all right, maybe folks'll let it slide, say they understand. You go after his daughter, though? You just made more enemies than you'd believe."

Evan looked up at the man, clearly trying to find some balance between what the bartender and his brother had been telling him all along. "It's what we got to do," the kid said finally, not sounding nearly as tough as Ship knew he had hoped to.

"You ain't got to do squat," Ship said. "Except survive. You ask me, your best move is to hightail it outta here now while the other two are tied up. I ain't gonna think no less of you for it. You might have trouble sleeping, but you oughtta be having trouble with that, anyway. You brought the wrath of God down on yourself tonight."

The kid looked like he wanted to protest when Matt came stumbling out of the back room. It had stayed fairly quiet while the doc worked, mostly on account of the patient being unresponsive, but the look on Matt's face spoke of a bloody ordeal.

"He got it out," the older brother said. "Doc says he'll be all right. Just gotta rest." He fell onto the stool by Evan. "I need a drink."

Ship poured another beer and looked over at Evan, letting the words Matt had just missed linger in the air. "Looks to me like you boys need a new plan," Ship said, setting the mug down.

Evan looked at Matt, who had his eyes closed, his Adam's apple bobbing as he guzzled the drink.

"Lemme talk to somebody. Y'all lie low here till I get back," Ship said, wiping his hands and walking over to get his hat.

***

The sun was just coming through the office windows as Ship sat down. It had been a long time since he'd sat in this chair, not because he avoided the place, but because, well, if something ain't broke, don't fix it.

Very little had changed as far as he could tell, including the woman across the desk from him. It had been years since he'd last seen her, but she didn't seem to have aged a bit. Still straight and poised behind her papers. Still demurely aware of her beauty and when she could use it. Still hiding a dangerously smart mind behind her large dark eyes. They'd crossed paths, sure, but every time, he was thankful he had enough wits about him to keep her at an arm's length. Some things, though, just plain needed to be brought to her attention. And anything involving Chancy Rosman had been specifically requested.

"Early morning or late night?" Anne-Marie said, leaning back in her chair.

"Eh, what's the difference these days?" Ship said. He wanted to be relaxed, wanted to show the nonchalance this woman did, but he could never quite feel settled around her. Even after she'd been in the shadows for so long, he still had to wonder, what had she been doing all that time?

"The life of a saloon owner," she said. "It catches up with one after a while, I would imagine."

He wanted to point out that she was up as well, but whatever her reasons for being in the office already when he'd gotten there, he thought it was best to let her keep them to herself.

"It's been a long time since I've seen you," she said, picking up the conversation in his silence. "I'm not sure if this bodes well or ill."

"I'm not real sure myself," he said, figuring honesty was not just the best option, it was the only option. It felt like she could read his thoughts without him even needing to say them aloud.

She raised her eyebrows and made a "carry on" gesture with her hand.

"Well, you said you always wanted to know if anything about Rosman came up down at the 'Yard and I guess you could say a lot came up in the last day or so."

"Ah, the Carter boys," Anne-Marie said. "I thought this might occur. I don't suppose it's a wild conjecture to say that they were unsuccessful in their revenge."

Ship looked at her. Word traveled fast in Elkhorn, sure, but he'd only been privy to all this for about twelve hours. Back to the wall. He couldn't even have said Anne-Marie was still in town twelve hours ago. No, he thought. Word of her lighting out would spread. No news about her ever came up, but if she was gone, he felt like the whole town would've known before the dust settled. He nodded. "Unsuccessful would be preferable to what they done, I'd say."

"The Saunders boy, then," she said. "I had my suspicions. Unfortunate event."

"Not just for him," Ship said.

"I couldn't agree more." Anne-Marie leaned forward and folded her hands on the desk. "I'm glad to see we're on the same page. It's so much simpler to deal with a man who has some kind of sense in his head. If you'll allow me the presumption of barreling ahead, I believe we can save ourselves some time here."

She looked at him and, unsure what else to do, Ship motioned in a "go ahead" gesture.

"Thank you," she said. "If I'm imagining this correctly, the Carters rode out to the Rosmans' ranch last night, seeking to avenge their brother, reclaim their honor, some such rot, and were disappointed to find Mr. Rosman was otherwise engaged at the home of a friend."

"Well, now, that part I don't know," Ship started.

Anne-Marie waved a hand. "His whereabouts are something I take great pains to keep tabs on. Suffice it to say, I'm sure he wasn't at home. That being the case, it stands to reason Fred Saunders may've been on his way over either to keep company with the daughter, or perhaps he just had the ill luck to be passing by. Either way, some sort of dust-up occurred, and now not only have the Carters failed, they've poked a stick at the cobra."

"They tried to run off with the girl," Ship said.

"Oh." Anne-Marie sat back in her chair, resting her elbows on the arms and steepling her fingers. "Well, that fills in some holes there, doesn't it?" She looked up at the ceiling for a moment, thinking. "I assume you know where they are."

"Yeah." Ship shifted in his chair uneasily. This was the part he'd dreaded most. He was never sure how the woman would react to anything, and this was something that could go strongly either way.

"They're at the bar," she said. "No need to hesitate. Your face says it all. That's actually quite good news, Ship, so rest easy. Are they all in order?"

He bobbed his head from side to side. "'Bout seventy percent. Ernie, the middle one, caught a bullet. Doc got it out, sewed him up. Other two're fine, just waiting for him to recuperate."

"So they can do what?" Anne-Marie said. "I suppose they have grand plans of going back. But of course, that requires Mr. Rosman to sit on his hands and wait, which I believe we're both inclined to assume he will not." She thought for a moment, then looked at Ship. "Mr. Buchanon, do you ever wonder why you don't hear more about me?"

He shrugged, unsure how to answer.

"You don't need to be concerned. The answer is quite simple. I don't *want* people to know more about me. Think of it like this: let's say you have two apple trees in your yard. One apple tree gives you more than enough apples. In fact, you couldn't even make enough jams and pies and preserves to keep up with it in a season if you wanted to. In fact, you don't even really need the other apple tree. I'm sure canning isn't necessarily your top priority in a summer, but do you follow me so far?"

Ship nodded. He followed, at least as far as he could see what she was talking about.

"Excellent. Now, let's add a little more detail here. You get all the apples you want from the one tree, and not only is this good for you, its wonderful news because there's a hornet's nest in the other tree, and every time anyone tries to get close, they come back all stung up." She paused. "Do you need me to spell it out for you?"

"No, ma'am," he said, at least fairly certain. "Rosman is the hornet's nest."

"Precisely," she said. "What the men before me failed to appreciate was that there is more than enough in this town without going out and actively looking for trouble. The problem with those men was that, no matter how much they tried to ignore it, the second tree still existed. And if there were apples anywhere, they wanted them all.

"I don't need all the apples, Ship, and I'd venture to guess that, given your longevity in a rather questionable business, you've made your peace with having one apple tree as well."

Ship nodded.

"I would almost guess no one's ever pointed that out to you, in which case, I'll be the first to commend you for it. It's a wise choice, my friend. And whether or not you know it, I believe that's what brought you here. Because those Carter boys aren't just in town. They're throwing rocks at the hornet's nest. And when the stingers come out, it will likely be more than just the three of them that need to run."

Ship hesitated, knowing the question was likely pointless but wanting to hear it from the woman before he committed. "So you don't think he'll settle himself with just the boys, do you?"

"I think when you try to kidnap any man's daughter, the rules go out the window. When that man is Chancy Rosman, everyone needs to be ready to run. After all, you and I both knew they were in town. They are all at your place right now, you said. You didn't go get Rosman. You fixed them up and came here." She thought for a second. "I suppose that's my doing, and I don't regret it. It's likely I would've been brought into the mix eventually anyhow. But as the problem presents itself currently, you need to put some distance between yourself and the Carters."

"You're going to send him after them, aren't you?"

She smiled. "Now, Mr. Buchanon, I'm not sure I care for what you're insinuating. What I'm doing is giving you the courtesy of privileged information. And it's not anything you couldn't piece together on your own. Rosman's going to find out who did this, if he hasn't already, and it won't take him too long to find out where they're holing up. Once he gets to you, whether or not you know it, he's going to come to me. We, you and I both, need those boys on the move. Where to? I don't care, but not anywhere near us."

Ship chewed on the idea, what there was of it. "I ain't saying you're wrong, but I don't think these boys're gonna just skip town."

"Then give them a plan. They don't have to skip town, they just need to have their feathers ruffled. Muss their plans. Get them moving anywhere, but get them out of the 'Yard." She paused for a moment and then smiled.

It could've been pretty on another woman, Ship thought, *but with Anne-Marie it was almost chilling.*

"Tell them to split up," she said. "Tell them their best bet is to keep him confused. Staying together gives him one target, separating gives him three."

"And the more they're out running, the more time they ain't with us."

"Exactly. The injured one, Ernie, you said?"

He nodded. "He'll be able to ride. Probably hurt like hell getting jarred around like that, but it won't keep his butt out of a saddle."

"Excellent. Just remember, when you tell them this, it's because it's the best plan and *not* because we're getting rid of them."

"Got it," Ship said, standing up. "You want me to come back around when it's done?"

"Not a bit." The woman smiled again. "We've been doing our business just wonderfully over the last few years and believe keeping our agreement is the right choice. If I need you, you'll know."

He nodded, wondering at her last words. He knew she was smart, knew she was informed, but perhaps he'd never really taken the time to think about just how far her reach went. "I'll take care of it," he said, walking to the door.

"Good man," she called after him. "Till we meet again."

Chapter 4
A Nervous Card Shark

Chancy was sitting across from Jack Wallace. Still, after the intervening years, he was slightly aware of the strange feeling of not being the one behind the sheriff's desk. Maybe it was just the difference in age, or maybe it was the fact that Chancy wasn't used to not being in charge of whatever he took part in. But for the time being, he pushed the thoughts to the back of his mind.

He'd spent the better part of the last few hours with Betsy and finally felt confident he had the entire story, or at least enough of it, to get Jack involved.

"I can't say the name rings a bell," the young man was saying to him. "Not that I doubt you, but you know how it is, Chance. Every group of brothers from here to Mexico likes to think they're the dread of the people."

"Yeah, I don't blame ya," Chancy said. "Truth be told, it took me more'n a few minutes to place the name myself. When I brung Bart down, though, there wasn't no Carter Brothers to it. It was just him out on his own. Tried to hold up a stagecoach down in New Mexico Territory, if I remember right. I wouldn't even'a known about him if he hadn't run up round where I was staying."

"Huh." Jack sat back, putting his boots up on the desktop. "Remarkable, isn't it?"

Chancy shrugged. "I guess it ain't part of the job anybody sits down and spells out for you, but, a fella'd be a fool to think he can run around like that and not have a few people wanting to come after him. I'd be lying if I said I wasn't surprised though. When Swally and them came through, it didn't take me completely off guard. But there hadn't been so many years between me and his kin. These Carter boys've been biding their time a while now."

"So you're sure then?"

"That's what Betsy said she heard." Chancy rubbed his hands on his pant legs. "I know she was in a right mess but that girl ain't one to get flustered too easy. 'He'll regret what he done to the Carter boys.' That's what she said she heard, clear as a bell."

"Sounds about right," Jack said. "They probably wanted to make sure she knew for… well…"

Chancy clenched his jaw. "I know what you mean, Jack. No sense in beating around the bush. I ain't broached the topic with Teresa much, but it doesn't take a schoolteacher to figure it out. We'd've gotten her back, eventually. They would've wanted her to deliver their message afterward."

Jack waved his hand in the air, as if dismissing the dark images from the room. "But they didn't, and she's safe, and if what you're telling me is right, at least one of them's got a bullet in him."

Chancy nodded. "Again, she wasn't sure on all the details, but she said she's sure Fred got one of them on account of the other dropping her to pick up his brother. How bad it was, I don't know. Seems too much to hope the Carter boys've been reduced to two already, though."

"Might be," Jack said. "Might not make much difference, depending on where he got hit. You said you took Fred to the doc straight away, right?"

"Quick as I could, anyway," Chancy said.

"Yeah," Jack mused. "I don't think them boys would've gone to the regular doc, anyway. One, because I don't reckon they'd've been familiar enough with the town to find him. Two, because they probably figured you'd be on your way."

"Or three," Chancy said, "they had somewhere else they knew they could take him."

"I been thinking that myself," Jack said.

"Only one sure-fire spot," Chancy said, "but it ain't any place you'd probably need to be going with that star on your chest."

"I don't know if it's any place for you to be sauntering in either," Jack said. "I don't think anyone's gonna believe you just finally went swing by the Shipyard on a whim."

"That don't leave us with a lot of choices."

"Maybe not," Jack said, "but you let me talk to a few folks today and see what I can find out. You remember the Nichols boy, Evan?"

Chancy laughed. "He was the first friend I made in this town. Even if he was just a pup at the time."

"Well, he's still doing what you asked him to way back then, except he's been talking to me about it instead. Even if you done nothing else since you got here, putting eyes and ears in the general store's been worth that boy's weight in gold."

"Ain't much of a boy nowadays, I reckon."

"You gotta get off that ranch more often," Jack said. "Point is, Evan's still doing like you asked, and I reckon if anybody's got an idea of what's shaking in this town, it'll be him."

Chancy nodded. "Tell you what…" He put his hands on his knees and stood up. "Maybe I'll just head on down that way and say hello. Like you said, it's been too long since I spent my time around town."

"Chancy." Jack stood up behind the desk, his hands on his belt. "You know that ain't wise."

Chancy had expected this, and despite agreeing with Jack, it burned him inside to feel like he was being left out of the hunt. "Jack, this is my family. I appreciate you wanting to follow the letter of the law here, but you and me both know it wouldn't be the first time we bent things to get done what needed done. You can't tie my hands on this one. I won't stand for it."

"I ain't tying your hands," Jack said. "I'm not even trying to protect you. We both know you wouldn't let me if I tried. But this ain't just you. They came after you, sure, but you saw what happened when you weren't there. The next best thing was good enough for these boys. You wanna know what I really think? I expect there was a part of them that was glad it was Betsy and not you. Ain't nothing for three grown men to pounce on a seventeen-year-old girl."

Chancy could almost hear Betsy's voice in his head, *Just for one more month*. She'd been so excited two days ago.

She'd been a happy, carefree young lady. Now, she lay curled up in her room, trying to sleep through nightmares so as not to face the ones waiting when she woke. "That's all the more reason I need to be out there doing something about it. I sit idle and I may as well put a sign up at the ranch. 'Come and take what you want. Chancy won't do nothing.'"

"Look..." Jack put his hand on the man's shoulder. "I get it that you're mad."

"Mad don't even begin to cover it."

"Yeah." Jack looked at him. "I reckon it don't. And that's good, but if you wanna do this right, you're gonna have to follow my lead on it. You wanna know the truth? I don't really care for the setup myself. But you just sat here acting like you hadn't seen Andy Nichols in five years, and the fact of the matter is you haven't, not much. When you moved out on the ranch, you took a big step back from all of us. And I don't blame you either. But you come back into town after something like this, you can put up a sign on the ranch. Except make sure it says, 'Here's the people to go after next.' Every person you go to is gonna be on the list, Chance. Evan's been good for us because he's discreet and most folks passing through wouldn't think one way or the other of him. Them Carter boys only know you're here. Everything else they learn is gonna be because you tell 'em."

Chancy socked a fist into his open palm. "You're binding me here, Jack. How'm I supposed to find out anything if I don't talk to folks?"

"You let me do the asking for you. Ain't nobody gonna think it's strange to see me wandering around town. Even if they know I'm asking about the Carters, well, don't it make the most sense that I'd be doing so? We had a boy shot last night. That's my job. What I happen to be asking, though, nobody's gonna know if those questions come from me or you. You already got some good info going here. I say you keep doing what you're doing. Talk with Betsy. Find out anything else you can."

"Jack, she's about talked out. You're making this harder'n it needs to be."

The young sheriff sighed. "I know it feels that way, but you gotta trust me on this. Maybe them boys figure you know it was them. All right. But that don't prove nothing. Not really. We can use that. If I'm the one they see handling it, it gives us even more room to move."

Chancy stood and looked out the front windows of the sheriff's office. This room was where he spent a lot of his time. He and Jack both had—some good, some bad—but always as a team, working toward a goal that, if he were being honest, he might not have accomplished if he hadn't had the younger man at his side. He looked back over at Jack. "All right," he said. "I can hang back, but like you said, they already expect you're gonna be involved, so ain't no sense in you and me being strangers. I need to know everything you do as soon as you do."

Jack smiled and sat back down behind the desk. "That's what I like to hear, Chance, because you're going to like this next bit."

Chancy looked at him and took his place back in the chair opposite. "Let's hear it."

"I know how we can keep tabs on the 'Yard without either of us ever setting foot there," Jack said.

***

Dinner at the Rosman house had been quiet the last few evenings. Betsy would come down from her room at least, go through the motions, but the process was slow for her. As well it should be, Chancy thought. There were so many factors to consider.

He'd done his best to explain to her she was innocent, just a person in the wrong place at the wrong time. He'd told her how she'd done the exact right thing in stepping outside and protecting the boys. He'd even apologized for his part in the incident, something she finally spoke up about.

"It's not your fault," she'd said. "Not exactly. I mean, sure, they wouldn't have come here if you lived somewhere else, but if we're just making up instances, maybe their brother would've if you hadn't tracked him down before. It's not our place to say what would or wouldn't have happened. We just have to deal with what did."

He'd put a hand on her shoulder that evening, impressed, as always, by the maturity the girl showed. Young woman, he thought. She'd been a girl when he'd met her, or at least as much of one as she'd ever been with her sass and smarts. Now her body was just catching up with her mind.

He thought about Fred again. The pair would've been a good match, though he wondered if Fred knew exactly what he was getting into with the Slayton women. They were delightful, to be sure: warm, smart, kind-hearted. But they were also tough when they needed to be, and for them, that had been often.

"I just wish…" Betsy had started, and Chancy knew she was almost reading his thoughts.

"Me too," he said. "But that young man showed some real guts. Riding down on three fellas like that." Chancy shook his head slowly. "He was a good one."

Betsy had nodded that evening, wiped an eye, and excused herself to go upstairs.

***

Now, sitting at the table, even the normally rambunctious boys seemed to have picked up on the feeling in the air. It wasn't tension so much, just delicacy, perhaps. Chancy had always been more of one to face his problems head on, track them down, kill them if need be. This was something different. It took some doing that he hadn't exercised in a long time.

Thankfully, Teresa had.

"Why don't you head on up to bed, dear," she said, looking at Betsy. "You don't need to worry about anything this evening."

"The boys," Betsy said, looking down at her plate.

"You may have forgotten," Teresa tried to be light-hearted, "but I know a thing or two about mothering. Chancy and I can handle the dishes and the boys and anything else needs done this evening. Your only chore is getting some rest."

"Thank you," Betsy said softly, slipping away from the table and up to her bedroom.

After a moment, Chancy looked at Teresa. "Think she'll be all right tomorrow?" The service for Fred Saunders was to be held in the morning, and while Chancy knew everyone in the Rosman clan wanted to attend, he wasn't sure if it was the best plan.

"She will be," Teresa said. "She has to be. I've made it clear the choice is hers, but do you really think she won't come?"

Chancy sighed. It was a tough thing, even for a man who had seen as many bodies as he had. On the job, it was just a part of things. People who lived the type of life he did knew there was bound to be bloodshed, more often than not usually.

Betsy was no stranger to death, having lost her own father so young. But that didn't mean it was something he wanted to put her through if he didn't have to.

"She'll regret it if she don't, I reckon," he said finally.

"It's the right thing," Teresa said. "That's all she's thinking about."

"Right and wrong aren't always so hard and fast."

Teresa looked at him, surprised.

"I just…" he started, unsure how to finish. "I guess I just don't want her going through it all over again."

"She'll be doing that whether or not you want her to," Teresa said, standing up and gathering the dishes. "It's all she's been doing. And I can't say I'm unaccustomed to the feeling. But the fact is that boy died for her. She'll be there. She'll be proper. And we will help her through it."

Chancy folded his hands, looking down at the table.

"The question is," Teresa continued, "when are we going to put this to rest? For good?"

"Hopefully sooner than we thought," Chancy said, then hesitated. "Look, Rees, I know you want to know what's going on with all this, but I was talkin' with Jack today and…" He trailed off.

"Let me guess," she said. "He wanted to remind you that anyone who knows you, who talks to you, who comes close to you, is in danger with this. Is that about right?"

Chancy nodded.

"Well, I hate to be the bearer of bad news, but that's been the case in this house ever since you stopped in so long ago. We're your family, Chancy. This is about *us* now, not just you. This isn't a bounty. This isn't just some other case. This is about what happened in our house to our daughter. I have the right to know. I demand to know." With a clatter, she sat the dishes on the counter and turned to him, her hands on her hips. The boys stopped their babbling and looked up.

"I ain't saying you're wrong," he said, patting the air with his hands. "And you've got a point. Ain't nothing I can do to keep y'all out of this one when it brought itself to the front porch. I'm just trying to figure how best to keep you safe."

"You know how to do that, Chancy. You've done that. You taught us to shoot. You rarely leave the property. But the fact is, there will always be the risk of times like these. We were lucky with Fred. So lucky I don't even like to think about it. But we need to know what's going on. I need to know. *She* needs to know that something is being done."

Chancy sighed again. He'd never been good at arguing with anyone. It was one reason the solitary life of a bounty hunter had been so appealing. But with Teresa, he really stood no chance at all. The woman was tough as nails when she needed to be.

"All right," he said. "Here's what I know. You're right on about Jack. He don't want me talkin' to anyone nowhere and nohow."

Teresa snorted. "Really helpful, that one."

"Now, listen," Chancy said. "Man's got a point. Ol' Andy Nichols is still keeping Jack abreast of things, but it ain't so well known as it was when I was sheriffin'. He seems to think if I start poking my nose around, the whole town will cotton on to the fact that I still got favors to call in and people willing to stick their necks out for me."

"Well, that's not exactly news," Teresa said.

"Maybe not," Chancy agreed, "but there ain't no reason to go about advertisin' it either. Now I'll tell ya, I warn't any happier about this than you are, but you gotta admit, he ain't wrong. And one thing we know is these boys ain't afraid to go after people close to me if they can't find me. I put that Nichols boy through enough years ago."

"And us?"

"You more than anyone. Don't get things backward here. But this damage is done. I can't undo what happened. You know if I could, I'd do anything to make it right. But the only way is forward. It's the only way we ever got. Moving forward, though, I aim to keep as many folks outta this as I can."

"So what's your plan, then? Just ride about? Kick over rocks and hope for the best?"

Chancy reached over to take her hand. Reluctantly, Teresa settled herself enough to let him. "Not quite that," he said. "We got us a fella who might help out, and he's got enough skin in the game to keep his wits about him."

"Ship," she said.

Chancy smiled. The woman was so darn quick. "Not quite," he said. "But you ain't far off, neither. Fella that hangs out about there. Named Jasper. Seems Jack's got something hanging over the kid's head about crooked cards or dice or some such rot. Ain't much really in the grand scheme of things, but the kid's young enough, he's still got a bit in him to scare. Jack says he ain't used him much, on account of the boy being so jittery. Said he's always half afraid Jasper's gonna crack if he pushes too hard."

"A nervous card sharp?" Teresa laughed. "He won't last long either way, if that's the case."

"My thinking exactly," Chancy said. "But whatever the case may be, the kid's willing to help. Shown he's willing to help, which is more to the point here. Jack thinks we can lean on him some and maybe get more outta the 'Yard than we would, even if I could go around talking to folks."

"Because who would really know anyway?" Teresa said, looking off as she followed the logic.

"Yep," Chancy said. "Them Carter boys came riding into town. They ain't got no connections. They ain't got kin here. They came for me and me only. Which means outside of Andy and a boarding house, ain't too many folks gonna see 'em, anyway."

"Just their bartender," Teresa said. "And from what I hear about Ship, he can provide the rooms and the supplies as well."

"You go it," Chancy said. "But Ship's been around so long now I don't reckon there's much left in him to scare. He's rolled through the last ten years without a scratch, which means he's either lucky or he's clever. I'm leaning toward the second one."

"Or connected," Teresa said.

Chancy let go of her hand, leaning back in his chair. "Y'know, that crossed my mind as well. And to be honest with you, back when McFarland was around, I'd'a said you were spot on. But between Jack and Mayor Travis, I don't see many options for backroom deals. Way I always figured was Ship takes care of Ship's problems, and now I ain't gonna say I prefer it that way, but sometimes it makes things a little easier."

"Until now," Teresa said. "Maybe he's not in anyone's pocket, but what leverage do you have over a man like that? It's almost like the town needs him around."

"Well, now," Chancy leaned forward. "That might be a bit much, but I ain't gonna say he's completely useless. If nothing else, he makes for a good starting point."

"And since you don't think he'll talk, it's onto this Jasper kid."

"That's the plan," Chancy said. "I can't shake the feeling Ship's been getting help from somebody, but whoever it is, we don't have even the slightest clue. Far as I'm concerned, for the time being anyway, there's no need to be shaking that tree. We use the kid to find out what we can, and then if things line up, we can go for Ship as well."

"If?" Teresa said, surprised. "This is the man who housed the Carters. He fed them. Gave them safe haven. He probably told them where we live, for goodness sake."

"Where precisely, I imagine you're right. But them boys ain't just been wandering about aimlessly. They knew I was here. They'd've found me. But don't think for a second that gets Ship off the hook. Jack may let it slide. Lord knows I did when I was in his position. But…" Chancy looked at her, his lips a grim line. "I ain't sheriff no more."

Chapter 5
The Grave and the Mine

The next morning, the preacher spoke his tired words over yet another casket claimed by the frontier. Chancy stood with his family, hands clasped behind his back, while Teresa balanced a child on her hip, an arm around Betsy who held the other.

Not much moved the man this late in life. It often felt like there was little he hadn't seen. But seeing something and being a part of it were never the same. The courage, the plain grit Betsy showed throughout the service, was more than admirable. He saw a single tear, quickly brushed away by the back of her hand, but otherwise the girl was a rock. A part of him wondered if it was for the best. Should he encourage her to have her feelings, to let go of the stoicism?

Then again, he thought, *there is no reason to pretend the West doesn't demand its people be tough.* And he knew better than to try to suddenly change almost eighteen years of upbringing. The girl knew herself better than he ever would. So he settled himself with being present, providing support in any way she needed it, even if that was simply to stand calmly by her side.

Mr. Saunders had made eye contact with Chancy a time or two during the service, and after the last words had been said and the crowd dispersed and intermingle, Chancy was unsurprised to see the man working his way over toward him.

Charlie Saunders wasn't a large man by any stretch of the imagination. He'd been wiry ever since Chancy had known him, something Teresa often tried to fix by sending over meals and extra baked goods, especially around the holidays. But no matter what she put in him, the man burned it off in no time. When Mr. Saunders grasped his hand and shook it, the grip was firm, an iron clasp.

"Walk with me, Mr. Rosman" was all he said by greeting.

Chancy spoke a few words in Teresa's ear, taking his leave for a few minutes, and walked off to the edge of the graveyard with Mr. Saunders. "A terrible thing," Chancy said, unsure how to begin.

"I won't mince words with you," Charlie said. "It is terrible. It's horrible. Something I wouldn't wish on my worst enemy. Though now, for the first time, I can say that the worst enemy has a face. Three of them, in fact." He paused for a moment, looking out into the distance. "I've tried to live a good life, Mr. Rosman. I've done everything I could to bring up Fred in the right way. Sure, he may've gotten into his tussles, perhaps caused more mischief than I got after him for, or maybe even knew about," the man seemed to smile just slightly at the thought. "But he was on the right track. I don't think it would be a stretch to say you knew that. Betsy knew that."

Chancy nodded.

"And I'm not foolish enough to think that life out here, life anywhere, for that matter, is easy. And it's certainly not something that is fair. A man does his best and hopes the good Lord takes heed. But we aren't guaranteed a single thing. Look at poor Job, for example. Do you know Job?"

"I ain't never been much for book-reading, even less for the hours spent in church every Sunday," Chancy said. "But I know my Bible well enough."

"I see," Charlie said. "Then you can understand my sentiment. Job did nothing wrong. In fact, they punished him for that very reason. A kind of bet between God and the devil. Well, I'm certainly not saying I'm blameless. And I'm not saying Fred was. But there's a difference here."

Chancy steeled himself for what he knew was coming, had hoped he wouldn't have to hear, because it could only mean more trouble. And that was the one thing he didn't need at the moment.

"You see," Charlie continued. "Job was an upright man. He was righteous. He stayed the course and continued to praise God throughout his trials and tribulations." Charlie looked at Chancy. "I'm afraid I can't say the same thing about myself."

"This seems like a matter you might wanna be bringin' to the preacher," Chancy said.

"It might, but I'm bringing it to you."

Chancy started to reply when Mr. Saunders held up a hand.

"I'm not turning my back on God. I'm certainly not feeling like He's the loving Father we've always been told of. But I'm not turning my back. In fact, I'm counting on the God of Job more than anything else right now. Do you know why?"

"He was a just God."

Mr. Saunders smiled. "Perhaps, perhaps. But I see nothing just about what happened to Job, or to Fred, for that matter. No, I'm depending on Job's God because He was a vengeful God."

Chancy sighed, looking off toward town to avoid the fiery gaze he could feel Charlie Saunders giving him. "'Vengeance is mine, saith the Lord.'"

"I see you do know your Bible."

The two men stood in silence for a moment, Chancy hoping Saunders was merely letting off steam, venting his anger out into the open to try to settle his soul. *But*, Chancy thought, *if it had been Betsy they'd just put in the ground...* he didn't think any amount of talking would bring him peace. "I know enough," Chancy said finally. "I also know they say God's time differs from man's time. And if you wanna know the truth, I ain't always been the most patient about that."

Saunders looked at him, the faintest smile on his lips. The man's face was haggard, worn. Chancy wondered if he had slept since Fred's death. His expression now was cold, calculating, a man looking for just the right tool for a very unpleasant job.

"I was counting on that," Saunders said. "I've tried to be a patient man in my days, but I must say, this situation doesn't allow me much in that area."

After years of being lied to and talked around, Chancy had learned a thing or two about listening when folks spoke. What he heard now wasn't what concerned him particularly, it was what he didn't hear. Charlie Saunders wasn't mentioning death, he wasn't mentioning the law or the lockup or the judge. He was putting distance between himself and what had happened. The Carter boys were a situation to be dealt with, no different from shoeing a horse or churning butter. Maybe not the most pleasant thing in the world, but something that had to be done.

"I ain't the sheriff no more," Chancy said. "I ain't even a bounty hunter. If I'm understanding you clearly, you need to rethink what you're planning. Ain't nothing but more grief gonna come your way."

"More?" Charlie laughed. "More grief? What else do I have to lose, Chancy? Fred was all I had left. What else could be taken? My home? Fine. Take it. Burn it to the ground. Everything I worked for was for that boy, so I could leave him a good life. But he's gone now. Do you see that? Everything I did has come to naught. It was fruitless. Pointless. The place can rot for all I care. But whatever happens, those boys won't be around to see it. And I want you to make sure of that."

"You needn't worry yourself about that," Chancy said, keeping his voice steady. "Me and Jack—"

"No," Saunders cut him off. "Not you and Jack. Not the judge. Not the law. I want those boys' heads. If you don't do it, I will."

That was what Chancy had feared the most. Saunders wasn't old, no older than Chancy himself. But he was too old to take up the life of a gunfighter, especially against someone half his age. Especially against these three.

"Look," Chancy said. "You may think you ain't got nothing left. It didn't serve no purpose. But you look over there." He pointed to Betsy. "That girl is alive because of your boy. The boy you raised. He done what was right because of what you taught him. You think he wants you going out and getting your own head blowed off for it?"

Saunders looked across the graveyard at Chancy's family, seemed to ponder them for a moment, and then looked back at the man. "If you don't do it," he repeated. "I will."

***

Jasper sat in the Shipyard's backroom, a deck of cards in his hand that refused to cooperate with his usually nimble fingers. The wooden table still showed the fresh dark stain from where the Carter kid had half-bled out on its surface not so terribly long before.

What they were doing, he couldn't be sure, but he knew if it were him, he'd be halfway to Chicago by now. Didn't make no sense to go out looking for trouble when it could find you easy enough on its own. And to go out looking for trouble with Chancy Rosman, well, that was just plain stupid.

He began dealing out a hand of poker to the empty seats around him, alternating between second deals and bottom deals as he'd practiced for years. Some days, most days, he didn't even have to think about it. Truth be told, giving him a deck of cards and asking for a fair shuffle would've caused him more problems than anything else.

It had been so long since he'd played a hand for fun, he really couldn't see the appeal anymore. It would be like listening to a song with your hands over your ears or going to a barn dance but sitting out every song. If you had the skill to really play, why not use it?

He reached out, naming hands before flipping over the cards to check his accuracy. He'd gotten them all but one.

Not bad, all things considered, but "not bad" had a way of leading to things he didn't want to think about.

A botched deal meant either you got yourself found out, and had to deal with the ones you were scamming, or you had to deal with the money coming out of your cut later on. Perfection wasn't just a goal, it was the only option.

He gathered up the cards, noting the top and bottom ones not because he intended to, but because he'd forgotten how not to peek. He worked through some simple overhand shuffles and false cuts, keeping upper and lower cards in their place.

He knew he shouldn't have talked with that Jack Wallace. But what was he supposed to do? When the sheriff is waiting for you, you stop. Besides, they had an understanding. Of sorts, at least. And Wallace wasn't asking for much. At least not usually.

A heads-up here and there, a few words to set him on the right track. Jasper was just thankful the lawman seemed to see more value in him than Jasper felt he was really providing. Sure, they had a deal, but any fellow stupid enough to walk into the Shipyard and think he was getting a square deal, whether it was cards, dice, or women, was a few kings short of a deck.

"The law's the law," he muttered, quoting the sheriff and riffling himself into a push-through shuffle.

"But it don't carry much weight here," a voice said, startling him.

The cards slipped between each other and his fingers, spilling out onto the table. He looked over to the door where Ship stood, his arms crossed over his barrel chest.

"Jeez," Jasper said. "You like to scare me half to death. I didn't think you was here."

"I'm always around somewhere," Ship said. "And when I ain't, you may as well just act like I am." The man walked into the room and pulled out a chair, picking up a card and flicking it toward Jasper. "You got something on your mind, kid? A fella talks to himself. I get worried. When he's talking to himself about the law, well now, that's something I feel I gotta take an interest in."

"Oh, it's nothing," Jasper muttered, gathering up the cards and squaring the deck. "Just that Wallace fella. I ain't worried about him."

"Maybe you oughtta be," Ship said. "You think I lasted this long by being tough? Only way to survive out here is being smart. You oughtta know that." He nodded to the cards. "Let's see what you got."

Jasper smiled. "What do you want?"

"Aces."

Jasper gave the cards a few shuffles and began flicking out four hands, with Ship sitting in the number three position.

"So what's this Wallace been on you about?" Ship said, glancing down at his first card and smiling.

"Oh, the usual," Jasper said, his fingers seemingly natural but going through a complex series of holds, breaks, and slips that, even when he knew what he was doing, he could barely see the sleights. "Wanted to know what's been going on with the games out here." He flicked out a few cards. "Wanted to know if I was dealing fair."

He flipped an ace across to Ship. The card was face-down, but he would've bet his life on it being the ace of clubs. "Man seems to think he's got something on me." He dealt out one more round of cards. "How's it look?"

Ship grinned, turning them around. "Looks like four aces to me," he said. "You might get too good at this, you know?"

Jasper laughed. "Now there's something I never thought I'd hear you say. Too good, huh? Bringing in too much money? Making your pockets bulge too much? That it?"

"Naw." Ship's smile vanished. "Not the dealing. The lying. I ain't no fool, Jasper, and I like to think you oughtta know that by now, seeing as how you basically growed up in this saloon. But a kid like you, there's always that one day he decides he don't need the old folks no more. Starts thinking he done fooled everyone else in town. Why not go for the whole shebang?"

Jasper leaned back in his chair. "I ain't been lying to you, Ship. I do my lying the same as the next guy, but I'd be a damn fool to do that to you."

Ship looked him up and down and slid the cards across the table. "See, this is the problem. I done taught you how to live by your wits and your words."

"And my fingers," Jasper grinned.

"Them too," Ship said. "And I reckon them fingers are mighty important to ya, given your choice of profession."

"Look, Ship," Jasper said. "I know you. I know where this is going. You ain't gotta threaten me or put the fear in me. I know which side my bread's buttered on."

"So what'd the sheriff want? And think about it before you answer."

"Like I said," Jasper straightened the deck again, thankful to have something to keep his hands busy. "Wants to know about the gaming over here, like he always does. He ain't getting a cut, is he? Ain't my business, I reckon, one way or the other, but I don't know why else he'd keep hounding me about it."

"Nah." Ship leaned back. "He ain't getting no cut. Not from me, anyway. What'd you tell 'im?"

"Same thing I always do. If he wants to find out about the gaming, come pull up a chair some night and I'll deal him in."

Ship looked at the kid for a second, then laughed. "To win or lose?"

"Whatever, it seemed like he needed to get him back out the door."

"That's good," Ship said. "That Wallace is slick, so if he keeps coming around, you let me know. It ain't exactly a secret what goes on out here, but it ain't exactly something he needs to be worryin' about neither. If he's sniffing after our tables, most likely he's heard something we ain't yet. So don't let him ruffle your feathers, but see what you can get out of him next time."

"You got it." Jasper felt his shoulders relax a little. "Call it."

"Royal flush," Ship said. He watched Jasper's hands as the cards moved and melded with one another. Whether the ones coming across the table were from the top, the bottom, or somewhere in the middle, it was impossible to tell. "There's something else we need to talk about."

Jasper felt his stomach tighten but didn't miss a beat with cards. It was a calming activity, in a way. He always knew where he stood with the fifty-two tools in his hand. They did what he wanted, when he wanted, and there was no second-guessing.

One day, he told himself, he'd light out of this town and set up shop where nobody knew his face. Maybe work a circuit, play the rube. It was risky that way, but the freedom had a certain appeal. Besides, if anything went sideways in this place, he'd need to find somewhere to go, and quick.

He eyed Ship over the table. What the man said next might be the first clue that the town was burned for him. "Hit me," the kid said.

"Them boys that was in here the other night," Ship said.

"Carters." Jasper flicked what he knew to be the king of hearts across the table and then reached over and tapped the bloodstain on its top. "Won't be forgetting them anytime soon."

"Well," Ship said. "You might need to be, least as far as your buddy, the sheriff, is concerned. We all know what they was here for, and we all know how bad they botched it."

"Couldn't'a done much worse unless that one feller'd died on us."

"That's what I been tellin' 'em, and that's what they're starting to think, too. But you don't just put out a fire like them boys got burning. I don't know when they're coming back. I don't even know if they are, but you need to make sure and let ol' Wallace know that, last thing you heard, they hightailed it outta town after things went south with the Saunders kid."

"They ain't gonna make it far till they're all healed up again."

"No, they ain't," Ship agreed. "What I'm hoping is, they're gonna take their time out there and reconsider their options. Hanging around here's just gonna get more bullets shot their way, and I don't have to tell you Rosman ain't one to miss." He paused. "You sure Wallace didn't say nothing about any of this to you?"

"Nah," Jasper said. "Just hounding me about the cards, like I said. Far as anybody in this town is concerned, I don't know nothing, and that's the way I'd like to keep it."

"You and me both," Ship said, looking at his cards and handing them back again. "But the longer you're hanging around out here, the less believable that story's gonna be. So I need to know we understand each other."

"Hey," Jasper said. "What happens to them boys ain't no business of mine. They came out here looking for trouble, and they found it. Ain't no different from anybody else riding after blood. It's why I keep to the cards. Less chance of catching a bullet."

"Not much less," Ship said.

Jasper cocked his head to the side and smiled. "Now that depends on who's holding the deck." Quick as lightning, he flicked four cards out onto the table. All four aces again.

"You're good," Ship said. "I ain't gonna deny that. But don't let yourself get too big for your britches. Don't matter how cocky you are. Them Carters were damn sure they were coming back to celebrate as well."

"I know it, I know it," Jasper said. "But I put in more time practicing than they did. It would appear."

"You better hope so," Ship said. "Everybody's luck runs out some day though." He stood up and walked to the door. "One more thing."

"What's that?" Jasper slipped the cards into his vest pocket.

"Want you to be my insurance on this thing. It ain't gonna take anybody too long to come sniffing around here about what happened to them fellas. I need you to keep your ears open. Especially when you're talking to Wallace. And if you see Rosman even turn this way leaving his house, you let me know about it."

"Sure thing, boss."

"Good. Because it's both our hides if something goes south. Now, listen. The Carters are holing up out by the old mine south of here. I told 'em they needed to get along soon as they could, sooner'd be better, but I didn't get the feeling they put much stock in what I had to say."

Jasper raised an eyebrow.

"Ah…" Ship waved a hand in the air. "Out-of-towners. All they know is what they heard, and somebody musta told 'em the 'Yard was safe. What they wasn't told was we don't keep their kind around too long."

Jasper nodded. It was a strange code, if one could call it that, but it was also an understanding. Killers came and killers went. Mostly a matter of circumstances and chance. Kidnappers though, especially ones riding off with a young gal like that. Well, they weren't gonna find too many friends no matter where they went. "You want me to keep an eye on them, I take it?" Jasper said.

"I ain't sayin' yes and I ain't sayin' no."

Jasper grinned. It was one of Ship's favorite phrases. Plenty of deniability, but always crystal clear. "I'll see what I can do."

"Look, though," Ship said. "You be careful. That lawman may be satisfied with what you told him for now, but if he takes it in his head to sniff more, you stay well away from that. We don't need to get mixed up in this mess."

"Sure thing," Jasper said. "I can take a ride out that way later on. I ain't ever had no set schedule no how. If'n I decide to take a wander south, it ain't gonna draw no more notice than if I went any of the other three ways."

"That's what I like to hear," Ship said. "And no rush. Just make sure you're on your own."

"You want me to talk to 'em?" He really hoped not. He'd seen enough of the Carters in the few hours they'd been around previously. Not a lick of class. And not that Jasper thought himself sophisticated, but he'd found a healthy chunk of his success by reading the people as much as by manipulating the cards. And what he saw in the Carters was the usual rabble. Loud, impulsive, and barely predictable. It was a combination that meant really only one thing that mattered: danger.

Ship seemed to mull it over for a moment, then shook his head. "Nah, nah. Them boys'll either go or stay. Whatever they decide, if they ain't gonna be swayed by me, they ain't gonna be swayed by you. Just keep an eye on 'em. If it looks like they're fixing to head out, let me know. If it don't, let me know that too."

"You got it, boss."

Ship nodded and walked back out to the main room of the saloon. Jasper let out a long, slow breath and ran his hands through his hair. If this didn't get Wallace off his back, nothing would.

Chapter 6
Trails

Chancy folded his hands and rested his elbows on the chair in Jack Wallace's office. "You're sure?"

Jack shrugged. "I can't say I'm sure. All I can tell you is what he told me, and Jasper said that's where Ship told him."

Chancy looked out the window of the sheriff's station. "You trust the kid?"

Jack shrugged again. "You know the type well as I do. He's what we got, though. Do I trust that's what Ship told him? Yeah, I do."

"But do we trust Ship?" Chancy said.

"That there is the rub," Jack said. "Way I see it, we got about a good shot of this being solid. I mean, put yourself in the Carter boys' boots. Which way would you go?"

"Depends on what I was looking to do," Chancy said. "And which one I was. Betsy said at least one of 'em caught a bullet, and what your boy Jasper says lines up there. Assuming he warn't just exaggerating to make hisself sound better, that means they're a man down. Least for the time being. So am I looking to lie low and come back or hightail it out of town?"

"Depending on how bad he is, could be both. Mine's been closed down since before you came into town, so maybe they're just looking to keep alive for now. It'd make a good place to stay outta sight, get the fella mended up, then head out."

Chancy rubbed at the back of his neck with one hand. "True. But it don't feel right. Besides, you get three boys fired up like they were, even if they was gonna leave, if they ain't yet, they ain't gonna. Not till they get what they came for."

"Yeah," Jack mused. "I was kinda thinking the same thing. Boy'd have to be on death's door for them to linger any longer'n they have to."

"If they were gonna go."

Jack looked across the desk at his former boss. "That ain't what's bothering you, though, is it?"

"I don't know, Jack. Just seems off to me. Ship don't get himself involved in anything he don't either have to or want to. So what's his interest in these boys? If they're out at the mine, they're away from him. If they're anywhere *except* the 'Yard, he can wiggle out of it like usual. So why send Jasper out to babysit?"

"Kid said Ship just wants to know what they're up to. Tryin' to keep himself informed."

"Maybe," Chancy said. "Or…"

Jack put his hands behind his head. "You think?" He put his feet up on the desk and looked at the ceiling. "I don't know, Chance. Jasper's young, but he's smart. I think if Ship was putting him to the test, he'd'a picked up on it. The old guy halfway raised him. Why would he test him now?"

Chancy shrugged. "How long's it been since you started leaning on the kid? Maybe Ship didn't have no reason to test him till now."

"Well," Jack said. "You may have a point there."

"Tell ya what we should do. You stick around town. Keep doing what you're doing, don't raise no fuss. And whatever you do, don't even think about them mines. I'll head out that way of my own accord later on."

"I don't know, Chance. Even if it ain't me, it's gonna be pretty obvious somebody mentioned the mine. Ship's smart enough to figure I'd tell you if Jasper told me."

"Maybe," Chancy said. "But that still gives us some room to work in. Even if he does piece it together, he ain't gonna be able to prove I didn't just head out there on my own. Besides..." Chancy stood up and adjusted his hat. "Us bounty hunters get used to lookin' about in unusual places. And in this instance, I've got sufficient motivation to be lookin' in all the places I can think of."

Jack sighed. "All right. But just look this go round. I know you ain't one for taking in a whole posse, but it's still three to one, even if one of 'em's on the mend. You see what you can see and then come on back. I'll do my best to take care of Jasper, but at the end of the day, he's old enough to know who he's been palling around with all this time."

Chancy nodded and walked toward the door.

"I mean it, Chance," Jack called after him. "You got a long leash on this one, but that don't stop a bullet."

"I'll try to keep one alive for ya," Chancy said, stepping out. "Assuming there's anybody there but spiders."

***

Where Ernie Carter lay, there were plenty of spiders, but they were fairly low on his list of concerns. The old shack he and Matt had come to was a far cry from where he'd planned on spending his days after the Rosman work was done.

Now, out here on the north side of town in a little cabin that had more bullet holes than nails in the walls, with his shoulder burning and throbbing, and his brother pacing around like a caged animal, the spiders could take a flying leap, as far as he was concerned. He just wanted to get on the move.

Without Evan around, though, Matt refused to decide, and Ernie couldn't very well force him to do anything, at least not till he'd healed up some.

Matt stood at the window, still for a moment, looking out into the emptiness. "You know what I heard?"

Ernie groaned. Gossip was Matt's specialty, and while Ernie had to grudgingly admit that keeping an ear to the ground had come in handy more than once beforehand, he was hardly in the mood for tales. "I don't know how you coulda heard nothing," Ernie said. "We been stuck here."

"Fore that," Matt said. "Afore we even come into town. I was askin' around, y'know, trying to figure out what it was we was getting ourselves into with this feller."

"What all could you possibly need to know?" Ernie growled. "Man killed our brother. That's enough for me."

"Yeah, yeah, I know he did," Matt said. "But you don't just jump in a fight without sizing the feller up first. I was trying to figure him out. Find out where to strike."

Ernie sighed. At least, for the moment anyway, Matt wasn't banging on about when Evan would come back, when they would all figure out what to do.

The problem was, when Evan wasn't around, Matt acted like no decisions could be made at all. So no matter how Ernie tried to reason with him, Matt just plain refused to make a choice. If for no other reason than to avoid the same old conversation.

Ernie bit. "What'd you hear?"

"I heard that, some years back, this was when ol' Rosman first came to town, some bigwig had the place in his pocket. Townsfolk decided they didn't like it no more and asked Rosman to do something about it. Well, he tried, and the feller he was after wasn't too keen on it. So he hires this other feller, some traveling gun. Guy comes in up and grabs ol' Mrs. Rosman. Dragged her out to some shack to spring a trap. Except, Rosman showed up with half the town behind him, shoots everybody dead."

"Everybody who?" Ernie said, bored. "Sounds to me like he oughtta just shot the feller who run off with his wife."

"Oh, he got him," Matt said. "But that feller had others with him. For back-up like. Story I heard was Rosman didn't leave a one of them breathin'."

"That's the story round the campfire, is it?"

Matt shrugged and ran a hand down the splintered wood in the wall, touching his finger to the bullet holes. "That's the story round the campfire, and if I ain't mistaken, the story in this here cabin."

From where he lay on a pile of blankets next to the wall, Ernie looked around. Light shone into the room at odd angles, through pinholes, chinks, busted windows. It wasn't a farfetched explanation. Someone had gotten what he had coming in this place, that much was clear. "Well," Ernie said. "If that's what you heard, I hope you're right."

Matt looked at him.

"Lightning don't strike the same place twice. If this is where Rosman did the deed, seems like we're probably in the safest place we could be."

A small smile played at the corners of Matt's mouth. "Y'know, I hadn't thought of it that way." He paused for a moment, thinking. "You sure we shouldn't go try to track down Evan? If this is the best place, wherever he is ain't as good. Right?"

Ernie closed his eyes, willing himself to be patient. How many times did they have to go over a plan before Matt would just accept it? "In case you forgot," Ernie said. "I got a hole in my shoulder and a stitching job by a drunk, half-asleep doctor. I ain't got no business running around looking for somebody who's perfectly fine taking care of his own self."

"How long we gonna wait, though?" Matt asked. "Sooner or later, he's gonna come looking here, no matter what the lightning has to say about it."

His brother had a point. That was the worst part of the whole situation, sometimes. They couldn't just hide forever, especially in the same place. Splitting up was smart, as much as he'd fought against the plan at first. It made them weaker as a unit but increased the odds they wouldn't be noticed.

Initially, he'd felt sure the old bartender was just trying to get rid of them, but as his body had begun to heal and his head cleared, he'd seen the smarts in it. Could very well be the only thing between them and a jail cell was the old bartender himself.

"It ain't gonna be much longer," Ernie finally said. "Evan's out getting the feel of things. Can't nobody sneak around like he can. Give 'im a few days. Everybody'll figure we done run off and we'll be in the clear. Till then, we just lie low. Not much else I can be doing."

"I reckon you're right," Matt said, walking away from the window and taking a seat on an old crate he'd dragged in to use as a chair. "You think we can trust that old man? Boat? Ship? Whatever his name was?"

Ernie shrugged with one shoulder. "Looks like we can so far. Way I figure, if he was gonna double-cross us, he woulda by now."

"Yeah," Matt said. "Yeah that's true." Then, after a pause, "I just wish Evan were around."

Ernie sighed for the hundredth time. "We *know* what to do, Matt. We been doing it. Lay low. Stay outta sight. Wait. You need to do somethin' so bad? Go out and see what you can rustle up for us to eat. I'm starving here."

"Yeah," Matt said, looking around the room. "Me too. But you know what they told us. Come nightfall, I'll go see what I can rustle up. Till then, we gotta be ghosts."

"You talk a hell of a lot for a ghost," Ernie said.

Matt shrugged. "Just tryin' to fill the time. Figure out what to do."

"You know what to do," Ernie said. "So do it."

"I am, I am," Matt said, getting up to pace the room again. "But still, don't you think I should go see the bartender? See what he's got to say?"

Ernie closed his eyes, hoping to feign sleep.

"That man ought ta know what to do," Matt said to himself. "He seems like he's got a plan."

***

"Yeah, well, that's the problem with plans," Ship said that evening. "Sometimes they work."

Across the bar from Ship, his other main cheat man, Marty, sat adjusting the spring tension on a holdout. They strapped the device to his right forearm and, as he flexed his elbow, a small set of metal pincers slid up and back. Most often, they secreted a card, but Marty had seen them work just as well, with only slight adjustments, should one need to tuck away a Derringer. "You're sure it was him? Not just some random fella?"

Ship laughed. "I appreciate you, Marty, I really do. You're always questioning everything. That's a good way to be. But sometimes you gotta take a leap of faith. And sometimes you can just believe your own eyes. I sat out there the better part of the afternoon and didn't see a damn thing, but sure enough, round about sundown, here come Rosman, big as the devil himself."

Marty used the head of a nail to tighten a screw on one joint. "I don't doubt ya there, Ship," he said. "I mean, are you sure it was Jasper sent him out that way? Everybody knows it pays to have Chancy Rosman owe you a favor. Maybe some kid just got a bright idea, threw it out there, and was hoping something would stick. Mine's a good hiding spot, and what've you got to lose, really? They're there, all right. Chancy gets what he wants, and he's got you to thank for it. They ain't, well, maybe they musta moved on 'fore he got out there to check on it. It ain't a bad play."

"No, it ain't a bad play," Ship said. "But it is sure one hell of a coincidence."

"Now that," Marty said, the pincers jumping back and forth along his forearm, "I will agree with you on. The question now is, what's next?"

"Y'know, I been thinking about that the whole ride back."

"Surprised you even thought about it that much. Anybody else'd have a bullet in their brain already."

Ship laughed. "Pays to be efficient. No use putting off tomorrow. All that. But then I got to thinking. Let's say Jasper is talking to Wallace. I feel like that's a safe assumption at this point. Agree?"

"Yassir."

"Well then, ain't there gotta be some way we can use that to our own advantage? Kid tells Wallace we're doing one thing, we do the other. He tells him we're going one way. We know all the others are clear."

"Makes sense," Marty said. "At least for a bit. Won't take Wallace long to figure out you're onto him, though. Then you still got Jasper to deal with."

"True." Ship pulled a bottle and a pair of shot glasses out from behind the bar, holding one up toward Marty.

"Thank ya, but no," he said. "Gotta work tonight. Can't be going in tipsy."

Ship looked at the bottle for a moment and then put it back. "That might be a good thing for all of us to keep in mind," he said.

"So what's the next step, then?"

Ship leaned on the bar, looking out over the empty saloon. It was early evening, typically a busy time for most of the eateries in the area. But the Shipyard wasn't a typical eatery. Their clientele didn't keep quite such predictable hours, though for many of them, this was just the beginning of the day.

He knew the smart move, but that didn't make him like it any more. Always the woman. It always came back to the woman. If the Carter boys were fixing to stick around, and Rosman didn't get to them first, Ship had half a mind to have them taken down himself, just for driving him back to the woman. Now, not only would he have to be seeing her again on account of them, it would be another favor he owed her.

But, he thought, *this time I have Jasper to offer*. Surely the woman would be happy to have her own rat to feed information to. Marty was right. It probably wouldn't last long, but it would be foolish to let an opportunity go to waste.

"You hold down the place for an hour?" Ship asked.

Marty looked around the empty room. "Yeah, Ship. I think I can handle it."

"Might not wanna be flashing the hardware while I'm not here watching the door, though." Ship gestured to the man's arm, but Marty was already buttoning the cuff, the device completely undetectable under the shirt sleeve. He paused for a second. "Whatever happened to just palming a card off?"

Marty smiled. "Gotta keep up with the times, Ship. See ya in an hour."

"Yeah," the man said.

***

"I can't say I'm surprised," Teresa said.

It was full night now. The rascals were in bed hours ago. Teresa was pleased to have noted that Betsy had gone up as well after finishing nearly all her dinner and actually engaging in some back-and-forth dialog at the table.

She'd tried not to let herself hope the girl would spring back quickly. Almost didn't want her to. Betsy deserved the right to mourn just like everyone else, and even if Fred hadn't been officially courting her, all the signs had been there that he was working his way up to it.

What had happened was just—she looked for the right word and then realized why she couldn't find it. The word was "unspeakable." And now, the first solid information they have about the men who did it, and it turns out to be nothing.

"Yeah," Chancy said from beside her. "I can't say I was, neither. But I had to at least see for myself."

"So where does that put us?" she asked. "The same place as before? Nowhere?"

"Not nowhere," Chancy said. "I'm just not sure where exactly. We know more'n we did before. It's just a matter of figuring out what it is we're supposed to do with it. Ship deliberately told that kid the wrong thing, just to see what he'd do. I can't say I'm floored by that move, but it's *what* he told him that gets me."

Teresa sighed. "Maybe it means nothing, Chance. What happened out here is the top gossip for now. Maybe Ship just used it for the test. He knew you and Jack would look for the Carters and figured it would be an easy way to see who he could trust."

"Maybe," Chancy said. "But it doesn't feel that way. I know you like your facts, and I can't blame you there. But I didn't make it this long in life by always waiting for the facts to come in. Sometimes you just gotta go with your gut."

"And your gut's telling you this really is about the Carters?"

Chancy gritted his teeth, trying to figure out what anything was telling him lately. "Yes and no," he said. "I think Ship knows something about what's going on with them boys. He had to, really. If he was gonna point us in one direction, he needed to know for sure that wherever we went, them boys wasn't there. And I went south. So I guess that leaves north, east, and west." He paused, looking out into the night. "Your gut telling you anything about one of them options?"

He expected a sarcastic remark, but Teresa surprised him by answering in all seriousness. "Why just one?"

"Well…" he started, then stopped. He leaned back in his chair, thinking about her words. "Well," he said again, "I reckon there ain't any reason it has to be just one, is there?"

"Three brothers, three trails. Makes it hard to track down any of them. I suppose it increases the chances you'll *find* at least one of them, but the odds are still in their favor. Two to one, no matter which way you choose."

"Maybe not," Chancy said. "The one that got shot, he ain't going nowhere on his own, at least not if he's wanting to last any time. But I think you're onto something here, Rees. They can still split up two ways. Now what we know is one of 'em is free as a bird. He can flit about all he wants to and keep ahead of us any which way from Sunday, assuming he's got enough of his wits about him to keep vigilant."

"Even then," Teresa said, "everybody's gotta sleep sometime."

"True, true," Chancy said, growing excited. "But that still leaves a pretty small window of luck for us to catch him when he ain't ready. The other two, though, wherever they went to, I'd just about bet you they ain't plannin' on lightin' out any time soon. I been shot a time or two, and that ain't something you just gonna spring back from."

"You don't say," Teresa said.

Chancy grinned a little. "They weren't too bad. The point is, instead of trying to find one brother runnin' all about tarnation, we need to just focus on the two that's staying put. Or is most likely staying put anyway. And now we know it ain't the mine they're holin' up in." He paused as he thought through his mental map of the town. It was detailed, much more detailed than he'd ever expected the first day he'd rode in so many years ago. Even so, it wasn't like that of a local. Granted, the Carter boys weren't local either, but if they had Ship on their side, they may as well be. He looked over at Teresa.

"You been here a long time," he said. "And so's Jack. We three put our heads together. We may figure out where them boys are staying."

"Maybe," Teresa said, the word coming out slowly, its length belying her thoughts being somewhere else entirely.

"What?" Chancy asked. "I been around a lot, but not enough to know every nook and cranny."

"No," Teresa said. "I'm not arguing that. But I'm thinking, if you really want to know where to hide out, where to cause trouble, where to go if you don't want folks to find you, would you ask the lady who used to run the boarding house and the sheriff?"

"Look, I see what you're saying, but it's better than nothing. And if you're thinking of Jasper, well, about the only thing we know right now is he ain't big on loyalty."

"No, no," Teresa said. "Think Chancy. You were a boy once. How hard would it have been for you to wander off if you'd wanted?"

In a flash, he grasped the image. It was clear as a day. "Are you sure?"

"To be frank with you, Chancy, no, I'm not. But I also think that, if we want our daughter back, maybe giving her the opportunity to help find the men who came after her would be a good way to start."

"You think she knows, though? I don't want to drag her into something for no good reason."

Teresa laughed. "After all this time, and you still think you can drag her into something she doesn't want to do."

He smiled. "You've got a point. But really? Betsy? When would she even have time?"

"I'm not saying *she* was out raising a ruckus, but if anyone would know where to do it, I'd about bet it would be someone in touch with those best at causing mischief. You find me a kid who doesn't know the best empty shacks and tucked-away caves, and I'll be impressed."

"Andy Nichols," Chancy said, grinning.

Teresa laughed again. "Andy Nichols was the one who probably told Betsy."

Chancy looked at her.

"He doesn't just talk to you. That boy's a wealth of information." She stood up. "For now, though, you wait here. I'll go talk to Betsy. The sooner we get to work, the sooner we can get back to normal."

Chapter 7
Dead Outlaws

"**S**hip, Ship, Ship," the woman said. "I've been seeing a lot of you lately. I can't say it's something I ever planned for."

Ship looked around Anne-Marie's office. They stacked files in boxes, drawers were open and empty. A pile of papers took up the seat in which he usually sat. "Looks like you're planning for something," he said. "You fixing to get outta town?"

Standing by the windows that overlooked the street, she put her hands on her hips and laughed. It was a sound he wasn't used to, and while there was a certain warmth to it, there was an underlying coolness that sucked any joviality out of the sound. "Are you worried I'm going to leave you all by your lonesome?"

Ship folded his arms. "I ain't too worried about much of anything you do."

"And yet here you are," she said. "You've made quite the habit of turning to me since your new friends arrived. Bite off more than you can chew?"

"First," he said gruffly, "them Carters ain't my friends. I'd just as soon be done with 'em. Bringing too much attention to their selves and that's leading back to me."

"And so…" She put a thoughtful finger to her lips. "Your brilliant idea was to come directly to me. That seems an awful lot like the pot calling the kettle black."

"I ain't bringing nothing down on you," Ship said. "Fact is, I'm wondering why I even came here. My intent, if you believe it, was to offer you a bit of a favor."

Anne-Marie raised her eyebrows.

"Or some information. Whatever you want to call it," Ship said. The woman unnerved him, and no matter how much he tried to steel himself before he entered her office, it never seemed to do any good. "Thing is, them Carters ain't been completely useless. Seems like they may've helped scare out a rat down at the 'Yard."

"I would've imagined there was more than one in that establishment." She rolled the chair out from behind the desk and sat down.

"I ain't talking about the critters," Ship said, trying to keep his tone even.

"Nor am I."

Ship looked at her, trying to gauge whether she was telling the truth or simply trying to get a rise out of him. He glanced at the chair again. Being forced to stand while she looked across at him reminded him of something he hadn't thought of in years: standing in front of the schoolmarm back as a boy.

It wasn't any secret he'd not pursued his education any longer than he'd had to. And he'd done just fine without the formalized rules and fancy words. But what he'd always remembered was how woman had looked at him years ago, like he was too stupid to be taken seriously and she could barely keep a straight face.

Anne-Marie wasn't quite so amused, at least from what he could tell. But it was close. No matter how much trouble he'd caused in the schoolhouse, the consequences didn't amount to anything compared to what this woman could bring down on him. And perhaps the most intimidating part was that he did not know how she did it.

He never saw her out. Besides the assistant or partner or whoever she was in the front office, Ship saw no one else around the woman. He knew she was connected, but beyond that, he was realizing no one really knew anything. And perhaps that was the biggest problem of all. It don't pay to pick a fight if you don't know who you're getting involved with.

And that was what had brought him to her today. Marty had said it paid to have Rosman owe you a favor. Well, it sure couldn't hurt to have the woman owe him one as well.

"Look," he said. "I won't bother tellin' you a bunch of things you already know." He looked around and then gestured to the papers on the chair. "You care if I move these?"

"I do," she said coolly.

He paused, already halfway to picking them up, then stood, hooked his thumbs in his belt, and tried to stand comfortably. "You sure you're not going anywhere?"

She sighed. "I can't possibly see how that is any of your concern. I spend time outside of this little burg, believe it or not. I didn't realize I needed to report my comings and goings to you."

"Just surprised is all," he said. "Packing like this makes me think you're fixing to leave for good."

"Packing? Or is it sorting? Reviewing? Tracking numbers is the term they use back East. I love how it sounds. Maybe I'm tracking some numbers, Ship. Seeing who is in arrears, who needs to be contacted." She smiled. "Or maybe it's just spring cleaning." She paused for a moment, watching him. "You're wondering if your name is in here, aren't you? Don't be embarrassed. You should wonder. But I'll save you the worry. Of course your name is in here Ship Buchanon. You and everyone else in this town."

He tried to glance at a few of the sheets he could see spread around, but the writing was too small to read at a distance.

"It pays to know things, sir," she said, drawing his attention back. "Not just illegal things, not just 'bad' things, just things. All the things. And if I'm not mistaken, you were on the verge of telling me something you believe I might not know. Well, please, continue."

"Yes." He gathered his thoughts again. "It's like this. After them Carter boys come out by the 'Yard, I done like you said, and sent 'em off. I figured that was the end. They'd be outta both our hairs. But there are rumors on my end of town. Most of 'em don't account for nothing, but sometimes they do. And the one I was hearing was that old Jasper was spending a little too much time hanging around Sheriff Wallace. Getting more friendly than he oughtta."

"I've heard that as well," she said. "I assume you've talked to him about it."

"I did. Kid told me ain't nothing but the sheriff shaking him down about gambling, cheats, small-time stuff like that."

"But…" She raised her eyebrows.

"But I figure that ain't much to go on. Maybe he's telling me the truth, maybe he ain't. So I let slip that them Carter boys are out by the mine to see what happens."

"Ah," she said. "So that explains why you and Mr. Rosman were out there the other evening. I was a bit surprised at that situation. There were even rumors that the rat wasn't Jasper, but that it was you yourself."

Ship looked at the woman, mouth open, unsure whether he should be angry that she would accuse him of such a thing (but she hadn't, really, had she?) or keep his thoughts to himself when he was around someone who knew every step he took. "I ain't no rat," he said finally. "I just decided I needed to see things for my self. So I told Jasper that's where the Carters were, figuring Wallace would show up. Rosman coming instead seems just as good of proof to me."

Anne-Marie nodded. "I would agree with that. And so then, what did you do?"

"Well," Ship rubbed the back of his neck. "Nothin'. Part of me wanted to go back and wring the kid's neck and be done with it."

"But then you got to thinking," she prompted.

"I did."

"And you figured a dead gambler isn't worth much, but a live rat might be."

"That's right."

"And so you've come to offer him to me, is that it?"

Ship shrugged. "I guess that's one way to put it."

"How very thoughtful," she said, holding his gaze. "And what exactly did you have in mind for this… exchange, is it?"

That's exactly what it oughtta be, Ship thought. But now that he was in the room with her, he would be happy enough to just give her the info and get. She always gave him the feeling that he was doing the wrong thing, saying the wrong thing, somehow tightening a noose around his own neck.

"I warn't expecting nothing," he said finally. "Fact is, between the Carters and Jasper, seems we've got problems piling up, and I figured you'd be the one who oughtta know. That's all."

Anne-Marie looked at him for a second longer, her calm eyes making his stomach turn. "You did the right thing," she said finally. "This town is threatening to become more trouble than it's worth, and I appreciate having something to our advantage. What you decide to do with the boy is up to you entirely, though I assume the plan is to use him for at least some time before cutting him loose."

"That was my plan."

"Excellent. Seeing as how you're the one he knows and you're the one he thinks he's fooling, I'd suggest you continue to be the avenue of his information. My only request is that you keep me abreast of your intentions beforehand."

Ship opened his mouth, then closed it again. He'd been hoping for directions, truth be told. Maybe that was the exchange, information for a solution. And not that he couldn't handle the kid. It was that he didn't want to make a tight spot worse. Still, what choice did he have now?

He nodded. "I'll do just that."

"Much obliged," the woman said, leaning forward over her desk and busying herself with the papers there. "I will give you one piece of advice before you go, however. Whatever you're going to do, do it soon. The law around here the last few years has been rather more efficient than I prefer."

"It'll be done in a week," he said.

"Make it a few days."

"Yes, ma'am." Ship turned and headed out of the office, kicking himself inwardly. *Ma'am?* He'd gone in hoping for advice and came out cowering like a beat pup. And what would he do in a few days? He needed a plan. And it needed to be good.

***

After Ship had exited the downstairs door, Anne-Marie's assistant entered the office.

"I'm assuming you heard all that?" Anne-Marie said.

The woman nodded.

"Then I also assume you need no more encouragement that we finish our arrangements here promptly." Anne-Marie leaned back in her seat and sighed, leaning her forehead on her fingertips. "I suppose it had to happen sometime, though, didn't it?"

The woman nodded again. "You have another visitor from the 'Yard."

Anne-Marie cocked her head to the side. "Send him in."

When the young man entered, the woman looked at her assistant and laughed. "We're going to have to serve drinks here as well."

***

While Ship was making his way slowly across town and debating his rather unclear options, Chancy Rosman was laid out flat on his stomach, his eyes peering down at an old, ramshackle, bullet-ridden, but so very familiar building on the outskirts of Elkhorn.

It had taken the better part of the day to work his way up, but the lack of cover in the area was what, almost contradictorily, made it such a perfect place to lie low. The sight lines in most directions were fairly unimpeded, so once you were inside, you were fairly safe. Assuming you didn't need to go anywhere.

And that was what Chancy had been waiting on for almost three hours. The need for someone to go somewhere.

After the attack on Betsy, the Carter brothers had made themselves difficult to track down, and now that it appeared Jack's informant wasn't so well informed, Chancy had let the official law work from one angle while he took the other. Thankfully, his gut, or perhaps Teresa's, hadn't led them astray.

It was the most he'd heard Betsy talk since her violent night, and that had been worth it, even if this had panned out to be nothing at all.

"I've just never seen the need to bring it up," she'd said. "It's all just rumors, ghost stories. But ever since what happened…" Betsy had glanced at her mother, avoiding the details. "It's where the boys like to dare one another to go. They say the spirits of the men still abide there or something silly like that." She'd looked at her hands. "You know how boys can be."

Chancy had smiled. "Yeah, I reckon I've got some knowledge of that."

"I'm sorry," she'd started.

"No need," he'd said. "You're not wrong. And I was the one asking, anyhow. So that's the spot, huh?"

Betsy had shrugged. "I don't know. It could be anywhere. I mean, if it were up to me, they'd be off to Mexico or Canada or dead in a ditch somewhere."

Teresa had almost interjected here, but Chancy held up a hand. "You're right. It could be anywhere. But the fact is, considering I'm sitting here talking to ya, I reckon they ain't got what they come for yet. Seeing as how I don't plan on just twiddling my thumbs till they decide to show their faces again, I figured this is as good a spot as any." He glanced at Teresa and quickly added, "And your mother agrees."

"It's either there or the mines," Betsy had said. "Those are the two places people avoid."

"And it ain't the mines."

The girl had shrugged again. "It seems a little juvenile, if you ask me."

Chancy had laughed. "Well, we ain't dealing with doctors and lawyers here."

And that was what he was counting on still. The Carters had never been known for their intelligence. Shoot, even having brought one of them down and, in a way, bringing this whole mess on himself, even he had had a tough time remembering who they were.

Men like that were still boys in a lot of ways, and if they needed some place to hide out, well, they'd look for a hideout. A cave. A mine. An abandoned building that the ghosts of dead outlaws might haunt.

Chancy had another thing on his side as well: time. Most men, disciplined or not, have enough sense to keep quiet when they know they're being hunted down. But given enough time, everyone feels comfortable where they are.

They think the danger has passed. They become comfortable. And that was just what Chancy had been counting on. Not long after working his way up within earshot of the cabin, he'd heard it.

Voices.

No matter how many times he'd seen it, it still baffled him. But you put any man in an enclosure, you take away his ability to see great distances, and he thinks his voice won't carry great distances as well.

Chancy had overheard more conversations than he cared to remember because the men talking had been in a tent. Stupid but true. Some trick of the mind, he supposed. But whatever it was, once he'd settled in outside the shack, he'd been able to hear the Carters clear as day.

The only problem was there were only two he could distinguish. There was a chance the two of them sounded similar. What seemed more likely was the one Fred had shot didn't survive his wounds. The other two were hanging back now, plotting their next move. Or, he supposed, the third could be in there with them.

Or one run off. Any number of things could have been the case. What he knew for sure was that two men were in the shack and, as soon as he got them separated, he was going to make his move.

Thankfully, as the sun set, Chancy got his opportunity.

The voices had been through spells of liveliness and quiet throughout the hours he'd been there. Bickering, mumbling, talking about all kinds of things he could only partly hear clearly. All that mattered was one sound, though: the front door opening. Then, without the impediment of the walls, the words had become clearer, crisper.

"Yeah, yeah," he heard one of them say. "I'll be right back."

Chancy tried to flatten himself against the ground as much as he could. He'd approached from the side, the same direction Travis had so many years ago, he realized. And with good reason. There was no path approaching on this or any other side. The sun would cast enough shadows most hours of the day to make the terrain moderately useful as meager cover, and he could see the front door clearly.

Now, one brother—though having not seen them in so long and at such a distance, he couldn't tell which it was—stepped out, called back to the man inside, and half-heartedly shoving the door closed behind him, walked down the main path.

Toward what, Chancy couldn't guess. There was little of sustenance out in the area. But the reason didn't matter, just so long as he had enough time to move.

When the man was far enough out of view, Chancy moved up into a crouch, working his way in a quick run down to the side of the building. He did his best to muffle the sound of his movements. The glass in the windows had mostly been shot out on that long ago day, and what had remained had been broken by the boys Betsy spoke of. Plus, the quieter he was, the better his odds of hearing someone moving inside.

He came up to the corner of the building, breathing slowly, straining his ears. There was no light coming from inside the shack, no sound. Whether there were two brothers inside or only one, he decided this was the only good shot he'd have. What he knew for sure was that one of the two able-bodied Carters was gone, and that tipped the odds healthily in Chancy's favor.

He removed his hat and worked his way up under the window, risking a quick glance through the opening. The sun setting on the far side of the building threw most of his side in darkness, or at least enough for him to risk it.

Inside, he couldn't see anything. Most likely, whoever was left was bunked up against the wall directly on the other side of him. That or the man who just left had been plumb off his rocker and carrying on conversations with himself all day long. Chancy grinned, knowing even he wasn't that lucky.

He crept to the front door, casting a glance quickly back down the path, and seeing no one, pulled his guns and reached for the handle. It was all one motion, a smooth, almost blurred change from crouched outside to standing inside, guns drawn, eyes moving lighting quick around the dim interior. The heap to his right moved. A body, a person. A crate was in the middle of the room. A few bottles. And nothing else.

He turned his attention to the man laid out by the window, holstering one gun and using his free hand to pull the door closed behind him. "Which one are you?" Chancy said, keeping his drawn revolver pointed at the pile of blankets and clothes.

The man laughed, a wheezing sound followed by a dry cough. "I reckon you ain't as smart as they say," he said.

"How ya figure?" Chancy glanced out the front window and moved back into the room, attempting to obscure himself from the outside.

"They talk like you, some big boogey man. You know everything. Can't nobody get to you. And you don't even know who you're talking to."

"I know enough," Chancy said, feeling his heart rate pick up. He'd brought in scores of men in his past, but what he hadn't counted on was the personal aspect of this, of seeing the man in front of him who had attacked Betsy.

"Do ya?" the man said.

Chancy clenched his teeth, willing himself to stay calm. "I know I ain't a sheriff no more, and I think you're one of the Carter boys. I'm wondering if you're as smart as *you* seem to think you are."

"How ya figure?"

"Well, let's say you are a Carter. I can run you in, or I can shoot you dead right here. I reckon the outcome's gonna be the same in the long haul for you."

"And if I ain't?"

Chancy shrugged. "I can still shoot you dead. Just means I gotta bury a body and I'll be getting home later than I expected."

"What're you gonna shoot me for? Ain't nobody own this place."

"Don't matter why," Chancy said. "I think I know who you are. If I'm wrong, well, I'll find out later, I reckon. Way I see it is the only thing you got going for you right now is how long you can keep me from putting a bullet in your brains."

The man on the ground looked up at him, perhaps trying to ferret out a lie, a bluff. In response, Chancy cocked the hammer on the revolver. "All right, all right," the man said, holding up a hand. "It ain't gonna matter much one way or the other anymore, I reckon. I'm Ernie. Ernie Carter."

"Now we're getting somewhere," Chancy said, glancing over at the window again. "And that one?"

"Matt."

"Where's the third?"

"Ya got me, boss."

Chancy moved across the room, crouching down to look Ernie in the eye. "I don't know if you're thinking clearly. I only need one of you."

Ernie looked up at him, then reached over and pulled back the side of his shirt. "I don't know if you realize, but I ain't got much time one way or the other."

Chancy looked down at the wound. The stitches, though not amateur, were far from perfect. The bigger problem was the red puffy flesh around them. And the smell.

"I'm rottin' out," Ernie said.

"Looks like Doc was drunk."

Ernie held up his hand. "I was bleeding out at the time. I reckon he gave me a few days." He looked around and laughed. "Though I can't say I owe him much of a thanks."

"You come in with me. We'll get you cleaned up. See what a doctor can do when you aren't laid out on a bar top."

Ernie shook his head, smiling. "And then what? Lead you to Matt. You stick around long enough, and he'll be back. You want Evan? Well, I can't help ya there. I don't know."

Chancy looked down at him, considering his options. The man was right. The way that wound looked. Even if he could get Ernie back in town, the doctor would have a hard time doing much about it. Once infection set in like that, once the smell started, it numbered your days. Despite that, anything was better than lying on a dirt floor and waiting to die. Chancy was just getting ready to say so when a voice called out from the front of the cabin.

Instinctively, he ducked down, moving in a crouch over to the window. He peered up through the opening. The other brother, Matt, was making his way back from wherever it was he'd gone.

"Don't pay him no mind," Ernie said. "He don't know nothing. Hell, he barely even remembers the last time you came around."

"Where'd he go?"

The man laughed. "You see an outhouse around here when you come up? Where ya think?"

Chancy put a finger to his lips then, listening as the young man outside came closer, looking around the room to figure out the best way to take them both in without bloodshed.

Planning was all the further he got, however.

"He's in here, Matt! Shoot him! Fire! Run!"

Chancy hit the floor, lying out flat as the bullets ripped through the wooden walls. The kid may not remember him, but he knew how to take an order. Having eyes on the inside didn't hurt, though.

"Below the window! By the door!"

Everywhere he moved, Ernie called it out. Dirt kicked up around him, and splinters burst from the dry wood. Chancy made for the darkness of the far corner, hoping to ease into the small space and at least reduce the size of his target.

The guns roared outside and inside. Chancy counted. Nine shots. Ten.

He stayed quiet, unmoving. He looked across the dusty room toward Ernie, who was now strangely quiet as well.

The seconds ticked by, and then one more shot ripped through the front door. Eleven.

A chill went down his spine. He'd never checked Ernie for weapons. His hands had been in the open, the blankets down at his waist. There wasn't a gun belt he could see. But that still left the surrounding floor, anywhere under the dirty covering. Before he could go after Matt, he needed to make sure he wouldn't get a bullet in the back for his efforts.

Chancy trained the gun across the room again, keeping quiet and keeping low. Odds were the brother outside was reloading or running, maybe both. And there was also that last shot. A misfire?

As the silence settled, Chancy could just faintly hear boots hitting the dirt, moving away.

Running away.

"Looks like you're on your own," he said, standing up and moving toward Ernie.

When there was no reply, Chancy moved more calmly, his expectations being confirmed. In the dying light of the day, he could just see Ernie's body up against the wall. A bullet had found his chest, another his neck.

Chancy thought for a moment, trying to remember. Had Ernie been directing Matt's bullets toward Chancy? Or toward himself?

He stood up and looked out the window. The brother was long gone, or at least gone enough that trying to track him down in the dark and alone would ask for more trouble than it was worth.

A scared kid will run until he's cornered. Then you don't know what he'll do.

Chancy pulled the blanket up over Ernie's face and walked out the door of the cabin, keeping an eye on the main path.

Chapter 8
Knowing How to Read

Chancy found Jack Wallace just where he expected to, sitting behind the desk in the sheriff's station, an oil lamp burning while he scratched away at some paperwork. Jack looked up when the door opened and then, seeing his friend, gestured to the chair across from him, leaning back and stretching his arms over his head.

"Any news?" the sheriff said.

"One's dead," Chancy said, easing himself down into the old chair.

"Split up, did they?" Jack said. "I wondered. Which one'd ya find?"

"Ernie. One Fred put the bullet in."

"On his own?"

"No, no. He wasn't in no shape for much of anything. The other brother, Matt, was there with him. Not really sure which one was taking care of the other, to be honest with ya. That kid don't have a whole lotta fight in 'im."

Jack held his hands out. "So where is he?"

Chancy shrugged. "He'll turn up. From what I seen, they ain't exactly working out a master plan here. You recall that shack out a ways where they had Teresa?"

"Ah," Jack sighed. "That was on my list for tomorrow."

"Well, you can scratch it off now. I didn't get a lot out of 'em, but from what I can tell, them two didn't even know where the third one is."

"Evan?"

Chancy nodded. "Ernie was dying as it was. Old doc stitched him up but didn't get him cleaned out. Matt was out when I got there. He came back when I was talking with Ernie, who got all kinds of wound up, hollering this and that. Before I could get a shot off, Matt had emptied his guns on the shack and was hightailing it. Ernie was done living."

"Shot his own brother?"

"Yeah," Chancy said. "Don't reckon it was on purpose, but he plugged him twice." He pointed to the spots on his own body. "Figured you'd wanna send the undertaker out that way before the animals find him."

"I'll do that," Jack said. "More importantly, though, what's our next move? Ain't too easy to plan when all we know is there's two fellas running around angry."

"Angry and scared, more'n likely," Chancy said. "The younger one didn't stick around too long. But I been thinking about that. Way I see it, we could run around in circles for days looking for these two fellas and never even know if they're still about."

"You don't think they'd just take off, though, do you?"

Chancy moved his head from side to side. "Fellas like this, I really don't know what to think. When they was three strong and going after a teenage girl, sure, they think they're pretty tough. But now they're down to two, and I ain't even fired a shot. Matt don't seem like he's got the heart for it, though I reckon that means he ain't got much heart for anything. If he meets up with Evan somehow, well, they may make another move. But if you want my opinion, waiting around or looking under every rock out here ain't the way I wanna be living my life. I need this to end. My family needs it to end."

Jack sat quietly for a moment, thinking. "If I'm understanding you correctly, you're wanting to bring 'em to you. And I can't say as I blame you, but I don't know if that's the way I oughtta be going about handling this. I'm supposed to bring these men in, not set 'em up for an execution."

Chancy looked at him.

"At least not till the judge says so," Jack amended.

Chancy sighed and looked around the room. "You remember when them boys come through a few years back? Tried to burn this place down with me and you in it?"

Jack grinned slightly. "Yeah, something like that sticks in your mind."

"You were right there with me," Chancy said. "You stayed cool, kept your head. You done a lotta good since then, but that was the night I knowed you were the man for that star right there on your chest."

"I appreciate it, Chance, but what're you getting at?"

"I'm saying you didn't get rattled. You didn't take it personally. And that's all right. Most of the time, folks ain't after you because you're Jack Wallace. They got you stuck in their craw on account of you being the sheriff. What we got going on right now, this ain't about you. This ain't even about who's the sheriff or who ain't. This is about me being Chancy Rosman, and these boys ain't gonna be happy with anything else."

"I can't just let you shoot it out with them, though. You've gotta see that."

"I ain't sayin' you gotta do anything. But you got people who talk."

"Jasper?" Jack looked up at the ceiling. "I don't think we need to worry about him anymore. He was the one who sent you to the mines. For him to know something, he'd have to be someone these fellas thought it was worth talking to, and I think we've seen that ain't the case."

"Maybe it is, maybe it ain't," Chancy said. "Maybe he was lied to. Maybe he was just wrong. Lotta maybes and I put little stock in them. I do put stock in you, though, so I'll offer you a deal. You do me this one favor, and if it don't pan out, then all right. I'll settle in and we'll do it your way."

"Chancy, I'm basically telling these men where to get murdered."

"There ain't gotta be no murderin'. All I want you to do is let your friend Jasper know where I tend to be."

Jack sighed. "I can't do it, Chance. If this was any other situation, you know I'd've suggested it already. I know you ain't afraid, and I know you can hold your own. But this one..." He shook his head. "It's too close to home for you. Literally."

Chancy looked at the man for a long time, considering his options, but knowing Jack wouldn't be argued out of or into anything. It was an admirable trait, even if at that moment, Chancy wished like hell the sheriff didn't have it. "All right," Chancy said finally, standing up. "I said my piece."

"Anything else," Jack said, "and I'm your man. But I can't lead 'em to the slaughter like that. We bring 'em in alive."

"Y'know," Chancy said as he walked to the door, "I think that's kind of up to them."

***

On the other side of town, at the Shipyard, Jasper sat at the bar, a warm beer on the table in front of him. He'd been antsy ever since the deal with the mines hadn't panned out. It could mean Ship was just wrong, or it could mean something else entirely.

All he knew for sure was he had to keep acting as if everything was fine. When the pressure was coming from both sides of the law, though, it made sitting still more than a little difficult.

He breathed a sigh of relief when he saw Marty's reflection in the mirror, coming through the batwing doors and making his way to the empty stool beside Jasper.

"Running late tonight, ain't ya?" Jasper asked as his coworker settled in.

Marty shrugged. "Don't pay to keep a schedule when you're employed as we are. Last thing I need is somebody knowing where to find me whenever they please. Besides," he glanced over his shoulder, "don't look like too much is happening in here tonight."

Jasper looked back as well, then down at his mug again. "No. Pretty slow. Ain't hardly seen Ship all night either. Something don't feel right, ya ask me."

Marty laughed. "If everything felt right, we wouldn't be making any money. What's got in your head all the sudden? Surely it ain't nerves."

"No, no." Jasper shook his head. "Ain't nerves."

"That's good," Marty said, leaning in closer. "Because I been meaning to tell you, that Evan fella, I hear he's coming down this way."

Jasper looked over at him, all else forgotten. "You're kidding me."

Marty smiled, holding his hands out. "I can't say if it's true or not, but that's what I heard. You need to keep your ears open, friend. School may come to Elkhorn."

Jasper's hands worked the air in front of him as if holding an invisible deck of cards. "A center deal."

"A center deal." Marty slapped him on the back.

Just then, the batwing doors burst open and a haggard, wild-eyed Matt Carter entered the room. "Where is he?" he yelled over the din. "Ship! I need Ship!"

Jasper and Marty hurried over. Getting things settled and the Shipyard back to normal would be good. Learning a new card sleight would be great. But getting this man calmed down and out of sight was the only thing that mattered at the moment.

"This way, this way," Marty said, putting an arm around Matt, who quickly shrugged it off. "No need to shout. We been waiting for you."

This last sentence caught the man's attention. "Why?" he looked at Marty suspiciously. "You have something to do with this? Where's Ship? And where's Evan? I need my brother!"

Jasper hooked his arm through Matt's and directed him toward the backroom just as Ship exited a door on the upper level. Jasper looked up and, seeing the nod from Ship before he disappeared again, hurried his companions along.

The trio slipped into the back, shutting the door behind them. Marty quickly pulled off his jacket and tossed it onto the wooden table, mostly covering the blood stain from the last time the Carter boys had been back there.

"Did you know? How did you know?" Matt paced back and forth. "Nobody should've known. And then there he is. And now… now…"

Marty sat down in a chair at the table, tossing an arm over the back and crossing his legs. He looked at Jasper, making a go-ahead gesture with his hand.

"We don't know nothing, all right?" Jasper said, trying to get Matt's attention. "We didn't even know if you was still around or not."

Matt spun around. "Then how did he know? Hm? How did he know where to find us?"

"Who?" Marty spoke up. "Yer not talking any sense. What happened?"

Matt jerked off his hat and ran his hands through his hair. "Rosman! Who do you think? I step out for one minute, and the next thing I know, he's in there. Ernie is dead. Evan's gone." His eyes widened. "I gotta get outta here. What'm I doing?" He looked back and forth between the gamblers. "You gotta protect me."

Marty looked at Jasper again, eyebrows raised. Thankfully, Ship shoved open the door, interrupting the scene.

Matt turned quickly, then, seeing the man behind Ship, pushed past the bartender. "Evan! You're here! Oh, Evan, they got Ernie! They got Ernie!"

The youngest Carter took his brother by the shoulders and shook him briefly, but firmly. "Calm down," he barked. "I oughtta be ashamed of you, acting like this. You oughtta be ashamed of you. Get it together."

"He came outta nowhere, Evan. You don't get it. One minute we was alone, the next he was in the cabin!"

Ship looked over at his two best conmen. "You get anything out of him?"

"Rosman tracked 'em down," Marty said. "'Parently shot the other one. This one ran off, I guess. He's wanting us to either get him out of town or protect him. Or protect him while he gets outta town. He ain't been real clear on that part yet."

Ship turned back to the brothers. "Get him upstairs and calmed down. You two are wearing out your welcome here fast."

"Got it, boss," Evan said, grabbing his brother by the arm and dragging him toward the door.

Jasper walked over and latched the handle behind them, sealing the three off from the rest of the bar for the moment. "Where the hell'd he come from?"

Ship sat down at the table across from Marty and shrugged. "Showed up, same as his brother there. Though he made less fuss about it."

"When?" Jasper demanded. "They were out at the mines!"

"I don't know where they been and where they ain't been," Ship said. "To be honest with ya, I don't much care except now they're in here, and that I don't like at all."

"Well, get rid of them!" Jasper nearly yelled.

Ship gave him a disdainful look. "You best watch your tone or you might go with 'em. I can't say you're acting much better'n that young one yer own self."

Jasper tossed his hat on the table, taking a chair and running his hand through his hair, unconsciously mimicking the man he wanted to be nothing like. "Sorry, sorry," he said. "I just been keyed up ever since they came around. Sooner they're gone, the better, I say."

Ship smiled. "Now on that, my friend, we agree. Them boys bring far too much attention to a place I been trying real hard to keep off folks' minds."

"But they're staying here now?"

Ship snorted. "No, they ain't staying here now. The younger one was here when I came in a few hours ago. Talked his way upstairs and was waiting for me. He at least had the sense to respect where he was. This other one, though… I ain't got much faith in him."

"Ya gonna run 'em off?" Marty asked, looking at his nails.

"Y'know, I was thinking about that. Way I figure, we done tried to run 'em off once. They been out doin' who knows what in who knows where—"

"That's right," Jasper broke in. "You said they were at the mine and now all the sudden this one's talking about some shack…"

"I told you what I heard," Ship said, emphasizing the last word. "Don't really matter much if they were there or not, though, does it? I mean, they're sure in here now."

"Yeah, yeah." Jasper looked down.

"So, what I'm thinking," Ship said, "is we give 'em what they want. We hole 'em up somewhere, and then we don't keep so secret about it."

Marty chewed at his thumbnail. "Bring the law to 'em, huh? Seems risky."

"Yeah," Jasper said. "Who's to say we don't go shooting off our mouths, and then they tuck tail and run off? Then what?"

Ship looked at the gambler for a long moment. "You got a point, kid. All right. Here's the deal."

***

It was late, well past midnight, when Jack finally reached over to turn down the wick on the office oil lamp. Most nights, he would've left long before now, but quiet nights weren't always as often as he would've liked, and it seemed, more and more, when he had one, there was plenty of quiet work still waiting to be done.

His hand hesitated at the knob as he heard the rushed boot steps on the wooden walkway outside. He sat back in his chair and waited.

A moment later, Jasper rushed in, checking over his shoulder before pushing the door closed and flicking the latch. He moved to one window, looking out in either direction, then moved to the other, doing the same.

"You're this wound up. I don't reckon the latch nor that glass is gonna do you much good," Jack said.

Jasper turned around and then hurried over to the desk, digging in his pockets as he crossed the room. "Here." he dumped a handful of items on the table. "You want proof I'm crooked. There ya go. Lock me up."

Jack looked down at his desk. Dice, cards, tacks, wax, a regular mishmash of things that could've been picked up from Andy at the general store. "I'm gonna need a little more information than this," he said. "Why don't ya take a seat?"

Jasper looked at the sheriff and then rushed over to the windows, pulling the curtains closed. "Turn down the lamp at least," he said.

Jack was about to protest when Jasper came back and took his chair. The fear in his eyes was real. No matter how good of a gambler you were, fear was tough to fake. Jack twisted the knob down to a glow.

"Thanks," Jasper breathed out. "Look." He held up one of the dice. "I loaded this myself. These cards, I marked them all. Here's some of the stuff I used to do it. There's more, but I had to move fast."

Jack reached out and rolled one dice. "Four." He rolled it again. "Two." He looked at Jasper. "Really?"
"They don't land on a number every time," Jasper said, rolling his eyes. "That would be absurd. Imagine how heavy they'd have to be. Then you're constantly swapping out," he waved his hand and opened one of the decks of cards. He split the deck and prepared to shuffle. "Watch."

Jack watched the man's thumbs, his fingers, his forearms, then looked up. "All right."

"No wonder you don't bring us in. You can't even when we try to get arrested. Watch here," he pointed to the back of a card, "the corner."

He riffled through the cards again and Jack saw it. The complexity of the design hid it on each individual card, but when they were seen in rapid succession, a little mark could be seen dancing around the circles in one of the designs.

"Do that again."

Jasper sighed, running through the trick once more.

"And you can read it that fast?"

"I don't have to read it that fast," Jasper said. "I just have to see what you're holding. Here." He held out the deck. "Take five cards."

Jack obliged.

"You got nothing," Jasper said almost immediately.

Jack raised an eyebrow.

"Four of clubs, eight of clubs, nine of hearts, jack of diamonds, and a queen of spades."

"I'll be," Jack said, turning the cards around to look at them. "That's some trick."

"Yeah, well." Jasper shrugged. "It ain't worth much if you're dead."

"All right," Jack said. "You've got my attention. What's the story here?"

"You'll take me in?"

"I reckon there ain't no law saying I can't, seeing as how you're being so polite about it."

"Good," Jasper said. "I need somewhere safe, and this is the only place I can think of."

"I take it things aren't going so well with your friends at the 'Yard."

"It ain't that, at least not precisely," Jasper said. "More like things will not go so well real soon, at least not as far as I can see. Ship's trying to set something up, get your boy

Rosman to come out guns blazing, and it's looking like he wants me in the middle of it."

"You think he knows we been talking?"

"If he don't, it don't matter much. Rules down that way make a short list. Ship's always right. That's all you gotta know. Nine times outta ten, he treats ya all right, stays outta the way. But he don't share too much about what's going on neither, ya know?"

"You know your bit and stay outta the rest of it?"

"Exactly," Jasper said. "You always wanna know what's happening down there, and I'm telling you about the games right now, because that's what I know for sure. Anything else you may've heard, I can't say yeah or no on it. Until now. Them Carter boys are gearing up to have it out with Rosman."

"And how do you fit into this?"

"Ship said he don't trust 'em. They showed up once and he told 'em to get. They done showed up again, and he's had his fill. So now he's got this plan to get them and Rosman together, and no matter which way it comes out, he figures he can wash his hands of 'em. See me and…" He trailed off, then looked up at the sheriff.

"Let's just say another fella for now."

Jasper nodded. "Me and another fella was there when they came in tonight. Or at least when one did. Ship comes up with a plan for me to take the boys down to Marlene's at that end of town." He raised his eyebrows. "The, uh, boardin' house?"

"I know it," Jack said.

"Says to keep 'em there overnight, make sure they don't run off, then noon tomorrow, we'll put out the word on where they are and let whoever wants to deal with 'em, deal with 'em."

"But you think he's planning on putting out the word early?"

Jasper nodded. "That, or he's thinking one more bullet in a gunfight, ain't gonna get noticed."

"You don't think you're getting carried away? After all, if he don't trust you, why would he send you out on your own?"

Jasper sighed. "Look, Sheriff, I ain't sayin' I picked the best profession, not by a long shot, but I'll tell you one thing. You don't live long at the card table if you can't read the fellers sitting there with you. Ship ain't no gambler. You put that man down, and I'd take him for every penny in his pocket. You know why? Because he ain't got no bluff. Worse than that, he thinks he does. Whatever he thinks is plain on his face, and right now he's thinking I don't know no better."

"You're sure about that?"

"It's why I'm here." Jasper looked at Jack. "It's the one play he wouldn't never expect."

***

"You really think he'll go to the sheriff, huh?"

"I'm sure he will," Ship said. "That's why I told him noon and I'm telling you nine. That good-for-nothin' may try to sneak out before the shooting starts, but I figure this way, he's gonna be planning a couple hours too late."

"Whatever you say, boss," Marty said.

Chapter 9
The Gray

The sun had barely come up when Chancy heard a knock at the door. He'd been up late, trying to figure a way to track down the two remaining Carters, assuming they were even still around to track down.

If he'd been on his own, he would've simply been out searching until he found them. That was the problem with the old plans, though: he'd been on his own. Now, every time he stepped out of the house, there was a lingering doubt in his mind that he shouldn't be going anywhere.

The trouble found him, and it had found his family instead. But if he stayed at home, wasn't he just encouraging it to come back again? He wouldn't trade Teresa and the kids for anything in the world. But he certainly wished he could just cart them off for a while till things settled. And the problem with that was the same thing that had gotten him out of bed so early—if he didn't know where the trouble was, he didn't know where was safe either.

He glanced up at the stairs as he walked to the door. His gun belt was hanging on the back of a chair in the kitchen. He paused for a moment and then turned back for it. Trouble probably wouldn't come to his door at sunrise, and it probably wouldn't knock either, but it never hurt to be prepared.

He skirted around the edge of the front room, glancing out the window. Down the lane a ways sat a horse and carriage. Whoever it was had left their animals far enough away to not disturb anyone who was sleeping.

Odd. The edge of the window cut off any good view of the front door, but he could make out just a hint of a red bustle. He paused, surprised.

"Good morning," the woman said when he opened the door. "I apologize for disturbing you so early, but I thought this might be the best time, given the current situation." She held out a hand. "You can call me Anne-Marie."

"Chancy," he said, taking her hand and stepping out onto the porch. "Seems that name of yours rings a bit of a bell."

She adjusted a shawl on her shoulders against the cool morning air. "Hopefully not too much of one. I do rather take pains to avoid that." She glanced at his hips. "I also certainly hope you don't feel those will be necessary."

"I reckon that depends on what brings you out here this morning."

"So many things, Mr. Rosman, so very many things." She walked over to where his and Teresa's rocking chairs sat and gestured to one. "May I?"

"Be my guest."

"Much obliged," she said, adjusting her dress across her legs.

A few puffs of vapor moved out as she breathed, but she took her time, getting everything just right, then pulling at the cuffs of the gloves on her forearms before continuing. "I said that I hoped you don't know who I am, though I must admit that may be only a half truth."

Chancy leaned back against the porch railing and folded his arms.

"A man of few words, I see. Well, I admire that, to be honest. A man who can't keep to his own business often ends up meddling in that of others. And a man who meddles in the business of others often causes trouble for others. And we both know trouble has a way of following one around, don't we?"

"If you're implying you know something about them Carter boys, you best start talking fast."

"Ah, the Carter boys." She leaned back, resting her hands on the arms of the chair. "It's funny sometimes, isn't it? The way things loop and weave in on themselves." She looked out over the yard. "You really have a lovely home here."

"I ain't got all day, lady."

"No, that's quite true." She opened her clutch and pulled out a small pocket watch. "By my reckoning, you've got about three hours, give or take."

"Until what?"

"Oh don't worry." She smiled, closing her bag. "Nothing to get riled about. You've proven yourself more than capable over the years. I think we both know that."

"Then you know what I need to be hearing."

"I know, Mr. Rosman," she said. "I know more than you realize. And what that includes are many, many things you don't know. For instance, I'm sure you don't know what I have to tell you about the Carters, and while my name may be familiar to you, I'm becoming rather convinced that, other than a tickle in your ear or the back of your mind, you don't know exactly who you're speaking with. Now I in no way intend to reprimand you for something you were unaware of, but I will say, perhaps this is a moment for you to consider in the future. Everything isn't solved with bullets and bullying. There is something to be said for finesse."

Chancy sighed and pinched the bridge of his nose. "Whatever you wanna call it. Tell me what I don't know. Tell me what I wanna know. But if you're gonna sit here, make it useful."

"Ah." She smiled. "That's precisely what I intend to do. You came here. What's it been now, five, six years ago?"

He thought back. Had it really been that long? An image of Betsy flashed through his mind. Young, ornery, grammar-correcting Betsy. "Bout that," he said.

"I thought so," she said. "Because your arrival coincided nicely with a mutual acquaintance of ours. Perhaps you recall Frank McFarland?"

Chancy nodded.

"I thought you might. He had a way of making himself known, even when he wasn't the one making the moves, as I believe you experienced. I trust your wife is doing well. Time heals all wounds, as they say."

"Daughter is too, thanks."

Anne-Marie nodded. "You'll forgive me for not asking sooner, but, well, they're quite strong women. I knew they'd show their mettle."

"How is it you know my family?"

"It's a small town," she said. "And to get back to what I was saying, I make it my job to know things. I knew your wife would recover. It's why I know your daughter will as well. I knew you would bring down McFarland. It's why I wasn't concerned when Mr. Swally made his run for power here. A town like this, you can learn everything you'd like if you're simply willing to sit back and pay attention."

"And you been paying attention to the Carters?"

She laughed. "One can't keep an eye on every little thing. You'll forgive me if this sounds cold, but I think you've learned that here yourself recently. Think of all the men you've locked up or made enemies. You certainly can't be sure that you know where every single one is at every single moment. It's an impossible task."

"And that's your job?"

"Not at all. My 'job,' is to know people who know things. To keep an eye on people who see things. I listen to what they hear. Think of me as a harp player. Each string has its job. I just choose which one to pluck and when."

"The longer you talk, the more you're sounding like a spider in a web."

She looked at him, a slight grin on her face. "If that's what the moment calls for. A spider sticks to its web, though, and I'm afraid it's time for me to move out of this one and onto another, to bend the imagery a bit."

"Well, I sure appreciate you coming to say yer farewells and all."

Anne-Marie steepled her fingers and looked across the porch at him, her eyes cool and collected. He felt like she could see into him, see through him, like she was reading his thoughts as he had them and assessing whether he was worth bothering with. Whatever she had, if she even had anything besides fancy words and a long wind, was what he needed, though.

"Look," he said. "I apologize if I'm not so formal as you're used to, but the fact is you said your own self you don't like me knowin' who you are. You tell me you know my family. About my jobs. Well, some of that ain't exactly secret, but some of it ain't exactly public neither. I'm trying to keep my patience here, but you're making it tough."

"That's fair," she said after a moment. "I suppose after having watched you for so long, I feel like I know you in a certain way. I sometimes forget you haven't been doing the same. Mr. Rosman, a man rode into town not long after you arrived. Do you remember what happened?"

He thought back. "Well, if you're talking 'bout that fella outside the saloon, I'd say I do." He looked at her for a moment. "You ain't his sister, are ya?"

She grinned faintly. "No, no. Not at all. I didn't know the man from Adam, to be honest. But that was when I started watching you. I knew things would go one of two ways with us, even then, from that first day. I knew we would either be working together, or I would need to make sure our paths never crossed."

"And yet here you are."

"Here I am, breaking my rule, so to speak. Now you can believe what you will about me after I leave town, and I'm sure you'll have no shortage of stories to choose from."

"About the woman nobody knows?"

"About the woman only some people know. But you yourself should be familiar with the way a reputation can take on a life of its own. I can't control what you may or may not hear, and frankly, I don't care. I am here today to tell you my version of the truth and that will be the end."

"Your version?"

"It's all we really have, isn't it? Take your Carters. In their version of the story, you're the villain. In yours, they are. You killed their brother, and they want to avenge it. They attacked your daughter, and you want to do the same. I'm not here to have a discussion of morals or virtues. I'm here to make a deal."

"Sounds like you're here for a lot of things."

"But they all come back to the same issue. Just as all the threads lead back to the same spider. I'm going to be leaving town after I leave this porch, and I'm telling you…" She paused. "I'm requesting that you let that be the end."

"I see little reason to keep chasing you," he said, believing this woman had nothing better to do than waste his time.

"You will, however," she said. "You'll see many reasons. What I'm asking you to do is to ignore those reasons, ignore what you hear, and remember this moment where you are speaking with me directly.nodded. "All right."

"I mentioned Mr. McFarland and Mr. Swally a moment ago. I'm sure I don't need to remind you of who they were and what they did. They would claim they were businessmen, and I suppose, in their own eyes, that was precisely what they were. McFarland anyway." She looked to the side. "Swally left a lot to be desired. But the point is, in some ways, many ways perhaps, their business and mine had what one might call places of overlap."

Chancy straightened up, his hands gripping the railing. "You were in cahoots with them?"

"Not in the way you're assuming, I assure you," she blurted. "You might doubt that, but think for a moment and I'm sure you'll see the truth. When you took them down, you should've heard about me, correct? If I were so involved with their plans, why have you never seen me before? I live in a gray area with the law, sir. I won't deny that, but what I'm telling you today is that you need the gray area to survive. Just like the gray area needs you."

"You aren't talking a whole lotta sense, but I know which side of the law I live on."

"Do you?" she asked. "Are you not prepared to shoot these Carters dead on sight?"

"That's different."

"The law is the law, Mr. Rosman. You no longer wear the badge, and you seem to see some leeway in that, but you aren't a lawman, you aren't a bounty hunter. You're a rancher. And ranchers can't hunt men down and kill them. Yet here we are."

Chancy clenched his jaw, holding back words he knew would get him nowhere.

"I see you don't care for that, and I can't say I blame you," she said. "But it's a valuable thing to know who you are. I know who I am, Mr. Rosman, and I know what that requires of me. That's why I took the risk of coming here today. I believe I know who you are, and I am putting my trust in you to not let me down."

She reached back into her bag and pulled out a small notebook, holding it in her lap. "The Carters, or at least the two remaining, are currently in room three at Marlena's Boarding House. I assume you're familiar with the location."

He nodded.

"Now, before you take off, guns blazing, there are a few other things you should know. One is that they are prepared for your arrival, but the details get tricky here, so bear with me. Our mutual acquaintance, Ship Buchanon, has been aiding the young men to some extent since they've arrived. He's the man who arranged for their current lodging, and he is the one hoping to solve some problems of his own with this meeting.

"First, you may hear a variety of information about what is happening today. I've taken it upon myself to keep abreast of things and would like to inform you that, should you wait, you will not be made aware of the Carters' location until nine am this morning. I'm telling you now to give you the choice to do what you believe is best."

"How'd you hear that?"

"I listen to people who listen. What I didn't mention is how rarely I decide to share what I've heard, so please pay attention... if you decide to make your move, you should be aware there is a young man in Ship's employ, a gambler by the name of Jasper, who Ship is hoping you will either kill in the melee or he will murder during this dustup and then pin on simple crossfire. It is my understanding that it's likely Jasper will be in the room with the Carters, or somewhere very close by. Again, I leave the choice of how to handle this up to you.

"Finally..." She took the book from her lap and handed it to him. "There is this. I hope that, should the information on the Carters not be convincing to you, this ledger will be."

Chancy took the book and flipped through the pages. It was filled with row after row and column after column of numbers, red and black uniformly making their way across the full, neatly penned pages. "What is this?"

"That is everything that has happened at the 'Yard in the last decade, give or take a few months."

"Meaning?"

"Meaning, all those times you thought about shutting Ship down when you were the sheriff, all those nights you wondered how he was moving his money, keeping his people out of jail, all the times his 'low profile' kept him safe in the eyes of the law, all of that is over. That book, Mr. Rosman, is Ship Buchanon any time you want him."

"And you're hoping by giving me this, I'm just gonna let you walk out of here. That sounds an awful lot like a bribe."

"It does, doesn't it? Luckily"—she stood up—"as I've heard, you don't wear a star anymore. So now, this is an exchange between one person and another. Or as I like to think of it, a farewell gift."

He hesitated, looking from the book to her.

"Let's be honest, Mr. Rosman, if you truly want to find me, you're able to. I'm simply hoping you won't have that desire. Besides, us folks in the gray need one another from time to time." She made a gesture out toward the carriage and then looked back at him. "I wish you the best of luck, whatever you decide. I've quite enjoyed having you around."

She nodded briefly and then walked back out across the yard as the carriage circled in. When she reached its side, the door opened, a familiar looking young man stepping down to help her in.

He looked back at Chancy, raised a hand, and then climbed back up the steps, pulling the door shut behind him. Chancy turned and went back into the house, already planning his next move. As he opened the door, he almost barreled over Teresa.

"Who was that?" she asked.

"I'm heading into town," he said. "I know where they are and this ends today."

"How do you know?" She hurried after him as he moved around the room, gathering his things. "Chancy, what did she tell you? How do you know you can trust her and it's not a trap?"

"I don't," he said over his shoulder. "But she built a pretty strong case." He pulled his coat on and grabbed his hat from the peg. "You stay here with the kids. If everything goes well, I'll be back before lunch."

Teresa held her hands in front of her, wringing them slightly. It was an old gesture, one Chancy rarely saw, but one he was familiar with none the less. She was worried, but she didn't want to admit it.

He reached over and put his hands on hers. "This is my chance to end this, Rees. It'll be over before anyone even knows what happened."

She leaned her head on his chest. "Be careful, please."

He kissed the top of her head.

"And no more strange women at strange hours."

He took her by the shoulders and held her back so he could look at her. "I promise. Only strange women at regular hours."

She swatted at him. "Go. I'll be expecting you by noon. No later."

He kissed her again and rushed out to the barn.

Chapter 10
Marlena's

Halfway into town, Chancy met Jack riding out in the ranch's direction. He reined his horse into a walk and met the sheriff in the middle of the road.

"I was just coming to find you," Jack said, a smile on his face. "I've got good news."

Chancy grinned. "You gotta get up earlier than that, my friend."

Jack looked at him, then turned his horse around, and the pair headed back toward the sheriff's station. "How could you know?" Jack asked. "I've had Jasper at the jail all night. Kid wouldn't let me leave him alone."

"I been listening to people who listen to people," Chancy said.

"What kind of backward answer is that?"

Chancy laughed. "Not really my style, I guess, is it? Well, look, I don't wanna take the wind outta your sails. What's the kid got to say?"

"First off," Jack said, "if you ever wanted to crack down on the cheats out that way, we got our man now. He may've been off with the mine, but ain't no judge in the world gonna watch him with a deck of cards and not put the hurt on ol' Ship's business."

"That good, huh?"

"Chance, that kid fooled me even when he told me what he was doing to fool me. I ain't never seen an ace jump around so much in my life."

"You'll love this then." Chancy reached into a saddlebag and retrieved Anne-Marie's ledger. "It might convince that judge it ain't just the kid that's slick out there."

Jack held the bottom of the book up to his chest, holding the pages down against the wind. He rode in silence for a few seconds, only slightly aware of Chancy out of the corner of his eye. "Where in the world did you get this?" he said finally. "I mean, this is *every*thing."

"A recent acquaintance," Chancy said.

"C'mon now, you ain't gotta play 'em close with me."

"Tell you the truth," Chancy said, "I'm not even sure I caught a real name."

Jack sighed. "Well, we can deal with that when we need to. Whoever this fella is, though, he ain't got nothing to worry about. Somebody willing to put in this much work for us deserves a daggone reward."

Chancy laughed. "I don't think it would be well received."

"All right." Jack stuck the book in his own saddlebag. "That's all good, but for now, we got bigger fish to fry. The Carter boys are gonna make a move on you today."

"At nine?"

"No," Jack said. "Noon."

"Huh," Chancy said, almost to himself, a small grin playing at his lips. "Right again."

"This is some acquaintance. Off by a few hours, though."

"You said you got the kid in there with you?"

"Yeah. Says he's thinking Ship's working on killing two birds with one stone."

"He ain't wrong there," Chancy said. "Too bad Ship don't know he's one of the birds."

"How you figure that?"

"Easy," Chancy said. "You go down to the 'Yard. I go to Marlena's."

Jack sighed. "We been over this, Chance. I can't."

"You can't send them boys to be slaughtered, I believe, is what you said. And you ain't. Now look, Jack, I'm putting a lotta faith in you here. You're the lawman on this, so I can't go around you, but I'm asking you to step aside. We make a move on the Carters early and then go for Ship. You know he's gonna figure it out. By the time you get there, that book won't be good for nothing but a paperweight. Now I can go down to the 'Yard on my own, but I'm thinking me walking in that place and goin' after him would be like tossing a match in a powder keg. Them fellas know I ain't no sheriff anymore, and if I get myself killed, well, it's cause I had no business being there."

"And I get the feeling that ain't the way it'd go down anyway, is it?"

"Not if I could help it, no," Chancy said. "I figure I'd at least take a few of 'em with me. But that ain't really my style. Besides, I told Teresa I'd be back for lunch."

Jack scratched at the stubble on his chin. "You can be a real pain sometimes, you know it?"

Chancy nodded slowly. "At least we're on the same side."

"Well, you ain't wrong there."

***

It was just before eight when Chancy slipped around the corner of the building and hurried through the front door of Marlena's. The place was just as he'd expected, though he'd never actually set foot across the threshold before.

Boarding houses of this variety tended, like most businesses on this end of town, to not do much in transactions before the noon hour.

A small couch and a tired-looking armchair were the only furniture in the main room. A sleepy-looking man leaned on the counter across the back, playing a hand of solitaire on the wooden counter.

He glanced up briefly at the sound of the door, but showed little interest and no recognition at the appearance of his new patron.

"You're too early," he said, almost to himself. "We don't rent no rooms till four pm."

"Well, that's all right." Chancy glanced around quickly and, seeing no one else, approached the counter. "I ain't looking to rent a room. Just trying to track down a couple buddies of mine. Room three, I believe."

The man shrugged. "Maybe." He glanced up from his game, for the first time noticing the guns on Chancy's hips. "We don't want no trouble here. We're a clean establishment."

"I wouldn't dream of it," Chancy said. "I'll be outta your hair in no time."

The old man held up a finger, gathered his cards, and walked out the front door.

"Smart fella," Chancy said.

He moved over to the staircase at the side of the room, drawing his guns and keeping his eyes in motion. The place was quiet as a graveyard, most of the occupants having likely gone to bed, or more likely passed out, not too many hours before. Still, it didn't pay to count on, probably.

He stepped slowly up toward the second floor, keeping his back to the wall and avoiding any creaking from the center of the stairs. The rooms were situated with their backs toward the building's facade, the single hallway cutting along the rear of the building, its wall making up the back of the building.

Four rooms. It was a wonder the place even made enough to stay open. Then again, he thought, a place like Marlena's offered a few more amenities than a typical boarding house as well.

Chancy paused at the first door, listening. There was a faint snoring coming from somewhere, either in this first room or the second. If he was to get double-crossed, this would be the place to do it. One choice out of four and nowhere to run, every step taking him farther from the only exit. Still, the woman hadn't let him down so far.

As he passed the second door, he could hear low voices, muttering, whispers. He moved slowly, heel to toe, letting his weight transfer as he made his way to the edge of the third door.

Now, closer, he could hear them. If it wasn't the Carters, it was at least the only conscious guests in the building. He passed the door, taking an extra pace, and then crossed over, putting his back against the wall of the room.

The voices were too low to be discernable, even with the thin walls. But the tone was harried. Nervous.

Good, he thought. *You oughtta be.* He reached out with one arm, using the barrel of his gun to knock lightly on the door.

The voices ceased immediately. A few seconds passed before he could hear movement in the room, no doubt the men inside preparing as best they could for what they couldn't even imagine. A floorboard creaked as someone approached the door from the inside.

"Who is it?"

There was another flutter of whispers.

"Jasper? Where ya been?"

Chancy stayed silent, hoping they'd be foolish enough to open the door. There was no sense in trying the knob himself. The slightest jiggle would be enough to announce his intention and with the men already as keyed up as they were, he had no intention of standing in front of the door long enough for a quick trigger finger to bring him down.

"Who's there?" the voice called again, angry now. "I ain't askin' again."

Chancy sighed. There were always plans. Always moves. Always ways to try to outsmart the next guy and the next one and the next one. But sometimes plans didn't go the way you expected. "Aw, hell," he said to himself.

In a fluid motion, he crossed the hall again, bracing his back against the wall and bringing his leg up. Putting his weight behind it, he lunged forward, the heel of his boot connecting with the brass plate on the door and bursting the latch through the thin wood frame.

The door flew back, collided with something, and bounced forward again hard enough that its impact knocked it off a hinge. Chancy was already in motion, throwing his shoulder into the wood and shoving the broken door back again.

Letting his momentum carry him, he came in low, his eyes seeing everything. The filthy bed. The end table with its oil lamp. A pair of old boots on the floor. A body in motion, stumbling back, bleeding from the nose. The bed caught the man at the knees, knocking him backward as he tried to stifle the bleeding on his face.

The second was crouched low, back where the door would've covered him had it stayed on its hinges. He was unfamiliar, but his arms were out in front of him, a barrel following Chancy's movements, but just a split second too slowly.

Chancy fired, once, as he fell, seeing the bullet catch the man in the forehead, throwing him back against the wall before the deafening roar had stopped echoing around the room. Chancy already had his other arm crossed over his body, the barrel trained on the man on the bed.

At the sound of the shot, the bloody individual had curled up, scooting backward across the mattress, trying to lose himself in the room's corner. A gun belt hung, useless, off a post at the foot of the bed.

"Don't! Don't!" the man called, holding out a bloody hand. "I'm unarmed! Please!"

Chancy got to his feet, glancing over at the body in the corner. A scraggly beard covered the lower half of the face.

Lines around the mouth and eyes. This was Evan Carter. He looked over at the man on the bed.

"I reckon you must be Matt Carter," Chancy said, standing over the young man, letting his full height loom over him. "Seems we haven't been formally introduced."

The young man looked up between the splayed fingers of one hand. Blood, some of his own, some from his brother, speckled and dripped from his face. Chancy used the barrel of his gun to flick the kid's hand away.

"Nobody ever tell you to look at a man when he's talking to you?"

Matt moved only his eyes, looking at Chancy from the corners.

"Ain't got much to say, do ya?" Chancy put a foot up on the edge of the bed, leaning on his knee and using the gun barrel to gesture with. "Funny how that works. Last time me and you crossed paths, you was all kinds of ready to put a bullet in me. Seems like it oughtta take a man to do something like that, though. Now here ya are, cat got your tongue and everything."

He stuck the revolver in its holster and leaned down, taking the man by the face. It would be so easy, he thought, somewhere in the back of his mind.

So simple. This was the last one. The last dog to lay a hand on Betsy. It could be done now. And before lunch. He smiled grimly.

"Stand up," Chancy said, jerking the man to the edge of the bed.

"Sir, I didn't—"

"I said stand *up*."

Matt Carter stood in front of the man. The ex-sheriff. The ex-bounty hunter. The man who, simply, had a score to settle.

"Them your guns?" Chancy gestured toward the bedpost.

"Y-yes."

"Ain't doing you much good over there are they?"

"No. Sir."

"Well, hell. Strap 'em on. You come all this way looking for me. Don't go giving up now."

"I don't... I... Sir..."

Chancy reached out and put his hand on the man's neck, slowly tightening his grip. It felt right. It was what needed to be done. To protect his family.

"You came all this way," he said. "You let me kill your brother right in front of you. You let Ernie die. You been hunting me like a dog. And when you couldn't find me, you went after my little girl."

The man's pulse beat against his hand, and his throat clenched and fought for air.

"Now you got what you want. Here I am. Not seeming too great now though, is it?" He lifted, Matt going on up the tips of his toes, his hands grasping at Chancy's wrist.

"I oughtta put a bullet in your skull right now," he whispered. "Ain't nobody gonna know the difference. I'll put a gun in your dead hand and be on my way."

Matt Carter stretched his neck out, gasping for breath.

Chancy looked at him and slowly, slowly, lowered him back down, loosening his grip until he fell back on the bed, his own hands at his throat now, as if to ward off Chancy's.

The silence in the room was heavy, the breathing of the two and the sputter of the oil lamp making the only sound in the windowless room.

Chancy looked down at him. "How old are you?"

"Twenty," he coughed, rasping out the word. "Twenty-three."

"Twenty-three," Chancy repeated. "Fred Saunders was only eighteen. I reckon you didn't catch his name, though. You know him as the fella who came out when you was…" Chancy felt the rage coming back as he pictured the scene. "When you was on my property," he finished, fighting against the urge. "You shoot Fred Saunders?"

"*No!*" the word came out clear, crisp. "I never even wanted to come out here! I told them to leave you be! When you warn't there, I told 'em let's go back. But Evan said… Evan…" The man's chest hitched and heaved, fighting against the tearing in his throat and what was maybe the first time he'd been able to tell his side in a long time.

Chancy rubbed a hand over his face, squeezing at his temples. He looked down at the bloody man on the mattress. Twenty-three. A lot can happen in that amount of time, and yet it still ain't much in some ways. He shoved his other revolver in the holster. "C'mon. Get yer b"I don't think you got any business around them," Chancy said.

Epilogue
What's Not There

A few days later, Chancy and Teresa sat out on the porch. Betsy, to their surprise and relief, had come down that morning, saying she felt like she'd been cooped up too long, that she needed to get out and get some fresh air.

Neither of her parents said anything about it, but they exchanged a stunned look. It wasn't the request so much as it was the tone. There was a firmness returning, a self-confidence that had been missing since the attack that night.

"I'll take the rascals out," she said.

"You make it sound like you're house-training puppies," Teresa had said.

"Aren't I? In a way?"

And that's when she smiled. The first smile they'd seen in so long. Teresa looked down, immediately finding something to hold her attention on the hem of her sleeve. Even Chancy had taken in a deep breath.

He wasn't foolish enough to believe the girl would simply bounce back. But he also knew her well enough to know this wasn't a time for too much attention too quick. It would take time, but that was something he planned on having to give.

While they had occupied him in room three of Marlena's, Jack had rounded up the deputies he could and made a clean sweep of the Shipyard. Ship had been asleep upstairs, apparently completely without concern that his plans could go awry.

Chancy had taken Matt down to the station and, once Jack returned, left the young man to his fate.

What exactly that might be, he had given little thought. The Carters weren't exactly a topic of conversation he felt like bringing up when he was at home.

He watched Betsy sitting on the grass, playing with the boys, and caught a figure approaching out of the corner of his eye. The Carters might not be something he wanted to bring up at home, but that didn't mean it wasn't something Jack wouldn't bring to him. He raised a hand in greeting, walking out to meet the man halfway across the lawn.

"How ya been?" he said, holding the reins while the sheriff dismounted.

"Busy," Jack said, taking off his hat and hooking it on the pommel of the saddle. "And them boys ain't anymore for keeping the quiet than they were for keeping the peace. I wasn't never too bad in school, but you ever try to read a book that's only numbers when you got a dozen fellas hooting and hollering in the background?" He shook his head. "Worst part is my only other option is to take it home, and that's the last thing I wanna think about when I'm there."

"Yeah," Chancy said. "I know that feeling."

Jack smiled. "Now this ain't about that." He paused. "Well, not entirely."

"Out with it."

"Here's the thing," Jack said. "You remember that gambling fella I was telling you about? Jasper?"

Chancy nodded. "He been taking your money?"

Jack laughed. "I'm telling you. If that kid had been a magician instead of a card-cheat, I don't think it woulda hurt his income none. But, thing is, he ain't no slouch. He's been going through them books with me now and again, and he swears up and down there was someone else helping him out. Seein' the numbers, I'm inclined to believe him."

"And Ship ain't talking."

"Oh, he's talking all right. He talks plenty. Got a new story every day. First, he don't know nothing, then he decides he knows everything, and if I cut a deal with him, he'll help me out. This morning he was telling me I shouldn't be worried about him at all. Said there's some mysterious woman running the show." He shook his head. "Any story you want, Ship's ready to give it to you. But this other gambling fella, he's the only major player ain't accounted for. Seeing as how Jasper ain't got nothing to lose and something to gain, I'm inclined to believe him."

"He give you a name?"

Jack paused for a moment. "Michael? Martin?"

"Marty," Chancy said.

"That's it," Jack said. "You know him?"

Chancy shrugged. "Used to see him around now and again. Enough to say hey on the street. He'd be about Betsy's age, I reckon, maybe a little older."

"You see him again, you let me know. And tell him about Jasper. Kid's making a real asset of himself, and I reckon the judge'd be more'n ready to play fair if Marty's got anything worth adding."

"Speaking of," Chancy said, looking over at the kids. "Any word about what they're gonna do with the Carter kid?"

Jack sighed, leaning an arm on the saddle. "That's a tough one. I got some lawyers sayin' he ain't done nothing wrong. His brothers forced him into it. I got others sayin' it don't matter who told him to do what, he was there and he warn't doing a thing to stop it."

"Sounds about right."

"What do you think? You been a lawman long enough."

Chancy thought for a moment. "I never was consulted much on that end of things, Jack. My job was always just to bring 'em in. What happens after that..." He shrugged. "Don't matter much what I think, one way or the other. Far as I'm concerned, he ain't gonna step foot back this way, and that's what I was after." Suddenly, a thought crossed his mind. The coach. Anne-Marie. And the kid who'd held the door for her.

"What're you grinning at?" Jack asked.

Chancy shook his head. "Nothing, Jack, nothing. Just seems to me things have a way of working theirselves out." He started walking toward the house. "Why don't you come in for a spell? Take a break. That jail ain't going nowhere."

Jack looked up at the sky. "You know, that don't sound too bad at all. I don't mind if I do."

The men made their way back toward the house, chatting, laughing, enjoying the day, the people. And one of them was finally enjoying something that wasn't there.

It would take some getting used to, he knew, not feeling the weight of the guns on his hips, but it was a feeling Chancy was ready to learn to embrace. And besides, if he ever needed them, he knew where they were, oiled and tucked away in a leather wrap down in the trunk at the foot of his and Teresa's bed.

But not too far down.

You never knew.

The End

Thanks for taking the time to read this story. A positive review on Amazon would be appreciated.

More westerns are in the works.